KT-220-983

THE COURTSHIP

OF

KATIE McGUIRE

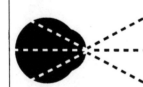 This Large Print Book carries the
Seal of Approval of N.A.V.H.

THE COURTSHIP
OF
KATIE McGUIRE

℘

JANE McBRIDE
CHOATE

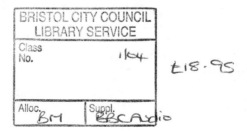
Thorndike Press • Waterville, Maine

Published in 2002 by arrangement with Jane McBride Choate.

Thorndike Press Large Print Candlelight Series.

The tree indicium is a trademark of Thorndike Press.

The text of this Large Print edition is unabridged.
Other aspects of the book may vary from the original edition.

Set in 16 pt. Plantin by Liana M. Walker.

Printed in the United States on permanent paper.

Library of Congress Cataloging-in-Publication Data

Choate, Jane McBride.
    The courtship of Katie McBride / Jane McBride Choate.
      p. cm.
    ISBN 0-7862-4582-4 (lg. print : hc : alk. paper)
    1. Fathers and sons — Fiction. 2. Single fathers —
Fiction. 3. Women teachers — Fiction. 4. Boys —
Fiction. 5. Large type books. I. Title.
PS3553.H575 C68 2002
  813'.54—dc21   2002072758

To teachers everywhere.
You are the real heroes and heroines.

Chapter One

Der Santa,
All I want for Christmas is a mom. I
kno I tole you I wannted roler blades and a
futball. But you don't have to bring me
any of that stuff if you bring me a mom.
                                        Love,
                                        Justin Chase

Justin stuffed the letter inside an envelope, sealed it, and marked it *Santa Claus, Noorth Pol.* He found a stamp in his dad's desk, stuck it to the envelope, and trotted out to the mailbox.

Dave Chase paused to swipe at the sweat pooling above his lip.

"What's the matter, pal?" Jack Carson asked. "You tired already?"

Dave punched his jogging buddy on the arm.

"Wow, would you look at that!"

Dave let his gaze travel in the direction Jack indicated, where another jogger had quickly outpaced them. Long legs ate up the paved track with an ease that Dave could only envy. He let his gaze travel up the length of her legs to encounter a compact body. Honey-colored hair, tied back in a ponytail, bounced against her neck.

She stopped and did a series of stretches. Stunned, he could only stare. She and his ex-wife Marie looked enough alike to be sisters. The hair, eyes, even the slant of cheekbones were almost identical. She looked to be about twenty-six, just a few years younger than Marie.

As if aware of his scrutiny, she raised her head. He continued looking at her, unable to tear his gaze away. The friendly acknowledgment in her blue eyes turned to quizzical challenge. She angled her chin.

Dave dragged his attention away from the Marie look-alike and forced himself to focus on what his friend was saying.

"Pretty, isn't she?" Jack asked.

"Yeah." Wincing at the hoarse croak, Dave cleared his throat. "Real pretty."

"Why don't you introduce yourself?"

Dave bit back a sharp answer. The last thing he wanted was to meet a woman who was the image of his ex-wife.

Jack clapped him on the back. "A single guy like you ought to get out more. Gives an old married man like me some vicarious thrills. Go ahead. She doesn't look like she bites."

"No." Hearing the edge to his voice, Dave softened it with a smile. "But thanks for the thought." Deliberately, he picked up his pace, effectively putting an end to any further conversation.

Behind him, Jack sighed. Dave ignored it and concentrated on completing the twenty-five laps necessary to make three miles. Though he pushed himself to the limit, the euphoria he normally felt when running was noticeably absent this evening.

The first hint of fall touched the air and gilded the leaves. The beauty was lost on Katie McGuire, though. Who could appreciate the gorgeous day when some man had glared at her as if she were a fugitive from *America's Most Wanted?* Even from this distance, she could see the hard light in his eyes. It was as if he'd disliked her upon sight.

Under other circumstances, she might have found him attractive. Tall and muscular, without being bulky, he had the air of a man who knew where he was going and how he was going to get there. For a moment, she found herself envying the self-assurance it must take to possess that kind of confidence.

Her own self-esteem had taken a beating within the last year. Dumped by her fiancé and laid off from her teaching job in Chicago, she'd decided to move to Canfield, Missouri, and make a new start.

She shrugged on the jacket she'd shed earlier and headed home, unable to put the man with the disturbing eyes from her mind. Obviously, not everyone in a small town was as friendly as she'd been led to believe.

Fall was Justin's favorite time of year. He liked the way the leaves turned all different colors and the way they sounded when he jumped on them. Sort of crinkly and crispy, like potato chips when he smashed them between two pieces of bread.

His dad had promised that they'd rake leaves on Saturday. Maybe he'd let Justin jump in them. Maybe his dad would even jump in them with him.

"Hey, Justin, wait up."

Justin turned around to see his best friend, Tyler Freeman, hurrying to catch up.

Tyler huffed to a stop beside Justin. "Didn't you hear me calling you? I've been yelling for you to stop for a whole long time."

"I was thinking."

"Oh."

Thinking was something they were talking about in first grade.

Tyler allowed a moment of silence before asking, "Whatcha want from Santa Claus for Christmas this year?"

Justin chewed on a fingernail. Normally he and Tyler told each other everything. But there were some things a guy couldn't tell, even to his best friend. Things like the letter he'd written yesterday. Things like how he sometimes cried himself to sleep because he wanted a mom of his very own.

More than anything in the world, Justin wanted a mom. He wanted a mom to come to school to pick him up when he got sick like he did last year when he threw up his milk and cookies after running too hard at recess. Of course, Grandma came and got him, but it wasn't the same as having his very own mom come and get him.

He wanted a mom to be there when he got home from school. Now, he went to his grandparents' home. His dad said they were lucky to have Grandma and Grandpa close by. And Justin loved them. He really did. They were great, even if they were sort of old.

He'd listened to other kids talk about

their moms. Sometimes they complained that their moms made them eat vegetables and yucky things like that, but he'd even eat *broccoli* if he had a mom. Though he'd suffer the worst torture imaginable before admitting it, he wanted a mom to tuck him in bed at night.

Tyler said his mom was always treating him like a baby, kissing him in front of people, calling him her "little man," and stuff like that. Justin never told Tyler that he wouldn't mind having a mom to kiss him, even if she did call him baby names.

It wasn't just for himself that he wanted a mom. That would be selfish. His dad needed somebody too.

He knew his dad loved him. Dad said Justin was his number-one helper. But sometimes his dad got lonely. The kind of lonely that grown-ups feel when they need another grown-up around, not just a kid. That's why Justin wanted his dad to get married again.

His dad hugged him all the time. Justin liked his dad's hugs, but sometimes he wanted a mom hug. Moms did things different than dads did. He didn't remember his mom very well. She'd left Justin and his dad when Justin was only two years old.

What he did remember, though, was how

she felt. Soft. Like his teacher. He knuckled away a tear. Dad didn't talk about Mom at all. Justin figured it was because his dad was still mad at his mom for leaving them.

Grandma told him that when moms and dads got mad at each other and couldn't work it out, they got divorced. He didn't like the sound of the word. It made him sad whenever he thought about it.

All that ran through his head as he thought about what to tell Tyler. Finally, he mumbled, "A bike."

Tyler gave him a look. The one that said, "Are you weird or something?"

Justin knew Tyler had gone through every toy catalog he could find, marking dozens of toys that he had to have, even though Christmas was almost three months away.

"Don't you want anything else?" Tyler asked.

Justin couldn't help the smile that spread across his face. "Santa Claus knows what I want," he said simply. "Hey, there's Mith McGuire. Let's walk with her."

"Nah. You go ahead. I want to play ball before school starts." Tyler headed off in the direction of the playground.

Justin hurried to catch up with his teacher.

It was a green apple kind of day, the air crisp, the leaves crunchy underfoot. A beautiful day, Katie decided, wading through ankle-deep leaves for the sheer joy of it.

On such a day, it seemed a crime to take her car to work, so she walked the ten-block distance from her apartment, not caring that the breeze mussed her hair or that she'd licked her lipstick off by the time she reached Walt Whitman Elementary School.

Fortunately, first-graders didn't care about such things. A smile turned up the corners of her mouth as she realized how much she looked forward to seeing the children every morning. They filled her days with laughter and surprises, like yesterday when Tyler Freeman put his pet white mouse in her desk. She had delighted the children by stroking the mouse and letting it crawl up her shoulder.

When Tyler had sheepishly put Mr. Hector back in his cage, Katie gently reminded him that animals were allowed in class only on show-and-tell days, and then only with special permission.

A field of pumpkins, just beginning to turn the bright orange of jack-o'-lanterns, covered a corner lot. White mice and pumpkins — all the ingredients for a Cinderella tale. All she needed now was a Prince Charming.

Well, she wasn't likely to find him in Walt Whitman, she thought. The only men who frequented it were old Mr. Tanner, the balding janitor, and Jeff DeHart, the sixth grade teacher, a happily married father of two with another on the way.

"Hi, Mith McGuire," Justin Chase, one of her kids, called as she neared the school.

"Hi, yourself."

"You look pretty." The blush that crept up his cheeks was the color of the maple leaves that carpeted the ground.

"Thank you. You're looking pretty sharp yourself."

His blush deepened.

She bit back a smile and offered one of the sacks she carried. "Think you could help me? These are getting sort of heavy."

His tiny chest puffed out. "Sure." He took the sack with both hands, gripping it tightly.

She matched her pace to his and tried to keep up with the myriad of questions he threw at her. Did she like little boys . . . even when they forgot to clean their rooms? Did she like to sing? Did she like to bake cookies? What were her favorite kind?

15

She answered each in turn with yes, yes, but she wasn't very good, yes, and chocolate chip.

Justin's smile grew brighter with each response as he followed her into the first grade room, making her feel as if she'd just passed some kind of test that she hadn't known she was taking.

She was about to ask him why he was asking so many questions but was sidetracked by a message over the intercom for her to come to the office. By the time she returned, it was time to start passing out the seat work.

With Justin's help, she distributed the pictures of a pumpkin and cornstalks that the class would color that morning.

Tongue caught between his teeth, Justin concentrated on his task, carefully centering the papers on desks.

Katie allowed her smile out of hiding. Moments like these made a teacher's long hours and low pay worthwhile.

She slipped an arm around his shoulders and hugged him lightly. "Thank you, Justin."

He leaned against her, warm and smelling of fresh air and sunshine. She clasped him close for a heartbeat before releasing him.

"You're welcome," he said, turning the full force of his toothless smile upon her.

She resisted the urge to plant a kiss on his forehead, knowing that would embarrass him. She settled for squeezing his shoulder. She loved all her students, but something about Justin touched a special place in her heart.

Maybe it was the way he managed to mispronounce her name and still make it sound like music. Maybe it was the way the freckles danced across his nose when he smiled. Maybe it was a lot of things.

She'd like to have a dozen children just like him of her own.

Back to Prince Charming again. He didn't have to be a real Prince Charming. She'd settle for an ordinary man who could make her feel extraordinary.

The ringing of the bell signaled the beginning of class. Daydreaming about Prince Charming was going to have to wait.

Justin had the mom picked out. Miss McGuire. She met all the qualifications he'd set out. She was pretty. She had happy eyes. And when she smiled, her whole face smiled. Most of all, she *felt* right. He'd known it when she gave him a hug this morning.

Miss McGuire was gonna be his new mom. Only she didn't know it yet. Neither did his dad. All he had to do was convince them that they needed each other.

Now all he needed to do was figure out how to get her and his dad together. He worried over it for the rest of the morning, so much so that Miss McGuire had to remind him to finish his seat work before lunchtime.

That gave him the idea. He chewed on his lip, going over his plan for getting them together. It was good, he decided. Real good.

He crossed his fingers for luck and took out his scissors.

"Miss McGuire, Justin Chase cut my doll's braids!" Emilie Taylor's wail cut through the clamor of voices.

Katie turned to look as Emilie held out her doll's blond braids. Katie knew the doll was Emilie's favorite, one she had brought for show-and-tell that day. Still, she had a hard time believing Justin was responsible.

"Justin, did you cut Emilie's doll's braids?"

Justin, holding a pair of scissors in one small grubby hand, looked down at the floor. "I guess so."

"You guess?" she asked in her best no-

nonsense teacher's voice. Her gaze softened as she took in the blond hair and dusting of freckles across his nose. "I have to send a note home."

"I know, Mith McGuire."

A smile slipped past her annoyance at the mispronunciation of her name. Two missing front teeth caused him to lisp occasionally — a common occurrence in a class of first-graders.

Her smile dissolved as she took in his cheerful expression. He didn't seem particularly upset over the prospect of having a note sent home.

"I'm going to ask your parents to call me," she said, hoping to make him realize how serious this was.

"It's just my dad and me. My mom's not with us anymore."

"How long has she been gone?"

"Four years."

Her heart ached at the quiver in his voice. Poor little kid. He'd been barely more than a baby when he lost his mother. "I'm sorry," she said softly.

"My grandma says Dad needs a new wife. She says he's in his prime and a man in his prime oughtn't to be alone. What does 'in his prime' mean, Mith McGuire?"

Out of her depth now, Katie became

brisk. "I'm sure I don't know. Right now, we need to decide what to do about Emilie's doll."

"Well," Justin said, clearly thinking it over, "I could glue the braids back on."

"I think that's a very good idea. We can do it during recess time."

"You mean I gotta miss recess?"

"That's exactly what I mean." *Along with my break*, she added silently.

The rest of the day passed without further incident. Justin managed to glue the braids back on. A wry smile touched Katie's lips as she wrote a brief note explaining to Emilie's mother what happened to the doll. Good thing that Mrs. Taylor was a veteran of six children. She'd probably pass it off with her usual good nature.

Katie's smile vanished as she wrote a second note.

"Please give this to your father," Katie said as Justin stuffed his papers inside his backpack.

"Okay, Mith McGuire." He tugged at her sleeve. "Mith McGuire?"

"Yes, Justin?"

"Are you mad at me?"

"No, honey. I'm not mad. Maybe a little disappointed, but not mad."

"I'm glad," he said, a grin stretching

across his face. " 'Cause I like you a lot."

She was struck by the sweetness of his smile and reached out to tousle his blond hair. "I like you too."

"A lot?"

"A whole lot," she said, a smile sneaking out despite her resolve to look firm.

"I'm glad you're my teacher."

"Me too," she whispered.

Dave Chase was running late. Seemed like he spent most of his life running these days. Running from home to Justin's school to work to his parents' home to pick up Justin and back home again.

He wasn't complaining. He had a wonderful son, a job he loved . . . most of the time, and great parents. Sometimes, though, he felt like something was missing.

A smile tugged at his lips. He knew what his mother would say. He needed a wife. She'd been telling him that for the last year or so. His smile died as he thought of Marie. It'd been four years since she had left them. Four years of trying to be both mother and father, trying to keep a business going, trying to let go of the bitterness he felt whenever he thought of his ex-wife.

"Dad, guess what? Grandma let me help make cookies."

Dave swung Justin up in his arms and gave him a smacking kiss. "Chocolate chip?"

"Is there any other kind?" Sally Chase said, wiping her hands on her apron.

"Nope," Dave and Justin said at the same time.

"Sit down and I'll get you a couple. Maybe you can get your dad to pry his nose out of the paper."

Dave grinned at his father. "How're you doing, Dad?"

Hal Chase looked up from the newspaper. "Not bad. Your mother's got a bee in her bonnet about us communicating more. Says I don't talk to her enough." He rolled his eyes in feigned exasperation before turning his attention back to the paper.

Hiding a smile, Dave picked up the sports section. His parents had been having the same argument for years, one he suspected they both enjoyed.

His mother placed a plate of cookies in front of him. He ate two and reached for a third, earning him a slap on the hand.

"Two's plenty for a man your age," she scolded. "You don't want to have a cholesterol problem like some people we know, do you?" She directed a knowing look at his father, who snorted in response. "That's why you need a wife. Someone to make you take care of yourself. Goodness knows, I've tried, but it's not the same as having a wife."

Dave glanced at Justin. The last thing he wanted was his son getting the wrong idea. "Mom, lay off, will you?"

"I just want you to be happy."

"I know. When the time's right, I'll find someone. Until then, leave it alone. Please," he added in an attempt to soften the order.

"You'd know best," she said in the tone of one who clearly believed just the opposite.

Dave exchanged a long-suffering look with his father. His father gave a sly wink before going over to kiss his wife's cheek. Despite their differences, or maybe because of them — Dave sometimes wondered — Hal and Sally Chase enjoyed a happy marriage that was going on its thirty-fifth year.

His mother handed Dave a note from Justin's teacher. The amusement faded from his eyes as he scanned it. He worried over it during the ride home, wondering what he was supposed to say to Justin.

Having a note sent home that his son

was in trouble at school wasn't exactly the end of the world, but neither was it something to cause him to cheer.

Dave had always thought he had a good relationship with his son, but tonight he wasn't so sure. Justin refused to explain why he'd cut off the doll's hair. In fact, he refused to say much of anything except to ask if Dave was going to meet with his teacher.

"I have to."

"Gr . . . I'm sorry, Dad."

Dave gave him a sharp look. Justin didn't appear very upset about the prospect. In fact, if Dave didn't know better, he'd say Justin looked pleased. The next moment he decided he must be mistaken. What little kid wanted his father to meet with his teacher?

The smell of school paste and poster paint assailed his nostrils as Dave found the first grade room the following afternoon. Children's artwork hung from clothespins, drying on a line strung from one end of the classroom to the other. He paused, studying the woman bent over a desk. A curtain of silky hair hid her face from his view.

She must have sensed his presence, for she raised her head and smiled. "Mr.

Chase, I'm glad you could meet with me."

"Mr. Chase?" she asked again, her voice a question this time.

There she was — the woman in the park.

Moving on autopilot, he crossed the room. Only when he came closer did the differences between her and his ex-wife make themselves known. He felt a sigh of relief shudder from somewhere inside him when he noticed the tiny gap between her front teeth, the full lips that were nothing like Marie's thin ones. Her hair, pulled back in a braid that fell over one shoulder, was the color of warm honey, the soft shade a distinct contrast to Marie's dyed blond.

"Miss McGuire, Dave Chase."

A faint wrinkle worked its way between her brows. "Have we met before?"

"Not really." He hesitated before continuing. "I saw you at the park a couple of nights ago. You were jogging."

Her frown deepened. "It was you . . . staring at me."

"I'm sorry. You reminded me of someone." He knew the excuse sounded weak, but it was the best he had to offer.

"Must not be a pleasant memory," was all she said.

"It's old news." He sensed she wanted to

25

ask questions, but she didn't. And for that he was grateful. The last thing he wanted to do was talk about Marie.

"Look, Miss McGuire, could we start over again?"

"Sure. And it's Katie." She stood and extended her hand.

"Dave." He grasped her hand, liking the feel of it. It was small but strong. Her nails were cut short and sported a coat of clear polish — another difference. Marie had always kept hers long and painted blood red.

Katie didn't wear a ring, he noted with surprise. Why wasn't a woman who looked like her engaged? Or married?

"Why don't we sit down?" She gestured to a child-size chair. "I'm afraid we don't run to anything your size."

He smiled. "Thank you." His smile dimmed as he remembered his reason for being here. "I'm here about Justin," he said, and immediately felt foolish. Of course he was here about Justin.

A frown puckered her brow. "Justin has always been such a sweet little boy. Up until yesterday, he never gave me a minute's trouble and now . . ." She paused. "Did something happen at home? Did you and he have an argument or — "

"Nothing's happened at home. What

about at school?"

"Aside from yesterday's haircutting incident, he seems happy. He always turns his work in on time, gets along with the other children, and participates in class. Maybe a little quieter than usual."

They talked for a few minutes more, with Katie promising to let him know if anything else happened.

On the way home, Dave had a hard time remembering he'd gone to see the teacher about Justin. He was having a hard time remembering anything but the way Katie's lips turned up at the corners when she smiled, and the dimple just to the right of her mouth.

Chapter Two

Justin had been on his best behavior for the last few days. He'd hoped that after his dad and Miss McGuire met each other, they'd realize they belonged together. When he'd asked his dad about Miss McGuire, all he'd said was that she seemed nice and they both hoped Justin wouldn't have any more problems.

Justin felt real bad about cutting Emilie's doll's braids off. He liked Emilie. Though he'd die before admitting it, she was all right . . . for a girl. She hadn't even screamed when Tyler put a rubber spider in her desk.

Maybe Justin could make it up to her for cutting her doll's hair. He'd have to think about it later. Right now, he needed to think of a way to get his dad and Miss McGuire together.

What could he do to make Miss McGuire so mad she'd have to talk with his dad? A frown puckered his forehead. He didn't want to do anything *really* bad. Just bad enough that his teacher would feel she needed to see his dad again.

Chewing on his lip, he pondered the question for most of the afternoon.

"Do you think Mith McGuire's pretty?" he asked, kicking a rock along as he and Tyler Freeman walked home from school. His grandma always said he'd ruin his shoes doing that. He wasn't sure what ruin meant, but it didn't sound good.

Tyler stepped into a puddle left by the recent rain. Both he and Justin watched in fascination as a worm inched its way across the sidewalk. "She's okay, I guess. For a teacher."

"Well, I think she's pretty. Real pretty. And nice too. She didn't even yell when Jennifer spilled her milk all over her desk or when you put Mr. Hector in her desk."

"Yeah. She's all right." Tyler cocked his head to the side. "You gotta crush on the teacher?"

Justin felt his face grow red.

"Justin's gotta crush on Miss McGuire," Tyler said in singsong before Justin could deny it. "Justin's gotta crush on the teacher."

"Do not."

"Do so."

"Do not."

"Do so."

They kept it up for the rest of the way to Tyler's house. Tyler poked Justin on the arm, hooting with laughter. "Wait'll I tell the kids tomorrow that you gotta crush on the teacher."

"You do and I'll tell them how you wet the bed when you stayed over at my house."

"Hey, I didn't mean nothing," Tyler said, his bravado slipping away, his expression anxious. "You won't tell on me, will you?"

"Nah. I won't. As long as you don't say nothing about Mith McGuire."

"I was just kidding."

"Yeah."

Tyler spit on his hand and stuck it out. "Deal?"

Justin spit on his hand. "Deal."

They shook on it.

Justin trudged the rest of the way to his grandparents' house. He wouldn't have told anyone about Tyler's wetting the bed. Heck, a guy didn't tell that kind of thing about his best friend. But he couldn't let Tyler tell the rest of the kids about Miss McGuire. It might get back to her. That would wreck everything.

Outside of his grandma — and she didn't count because she was old — Miss McGuire was the nicest lady Justin knew. She was always smiling, and she smelled nice too. Like sunshine and peppermints.

Sometimes she gave him a hug. Justin liked the way her arms felt around him.

When his grandmother asked him if he wanted to lick the bowl of cake batter, he shook his head. Normally, he loved scraping the bowl clean of batter that she left for him whenever she made a cake, but today he had bigger things on his mind.

The solution came that evening as his father tucked him into bed.

"Good night, slugger," his dad said, sliding Justin's favorite stuffed animal next to him.

Automatically, Justin wrapped his arms around Harry the Hare. Then it came to him. The idea was so simple, he wondered why he hadn't thought of it before.

" 'Night, Dad." A grin settled over his lips as he planned his next move in the campaign to get his two favorite people together.

Flushed from an energetic recess of jumping rope, Katie hurried back to her classroom. When the other first grade teacher caught her in the hall to compare notes about the plans for the Halloween party, she glanced at her watch. Finally taking the hint, the teacher let her go.

Something was wrong.

She saw it in the eyes of the children.

Heard it in the break of their excited chatter.

Felt it in the waiting tension that filled the classroom.

A quick scan of the room didn't reveal anything out of order. She repeated the process, taking her time. Her gaze faltered, then slid back to the rabbit cages. Maybe she'd been mistaken.

She hadn't.

Two plump white rabbits, a male and a female, stared affectionately at each other in a single cage. She'd made a point of explaining to the children when the class adopted the two animals that they had to remain in separate cages.

Was it her imagination or did the female one look slightly plumper?

Get a grip, she chided herself silently, barely repressing a sigh. Even if Mrs. Carrot Top were pregnant, she wouldn't be showing already . . . would she? Of course, Katie admitted, her knowledge of the mating habits of rabbits was limited to a few paragraphs in an encyclopedia.

She turned to face the class. The very quiet class. Only the nervous twitter from one of the girls interrupted the silence.

Katie planted her hands on her hips in

her best teacher fashion. "All right. Who put Mr. Whiskers and Mrs. Carrot Top in the same cage?"

Some snickers broke the unnatural quiet. A few heads turned in the direction of Justin's desk. Justin looked up, his gray eyes wide and a touch frightened, each freckle standing out in sharp relief against his fair skin.

"Justin, did you put Mr. Whiskers in Mrs. Carrot Top's cage?"

"Yes, Mith McGuire."

She didn't try to repress her sigh this time. "Okay, everyone. Back to work. Justin, we'll talk about this later."

"Yes, ma'am."

What were the consequences of a litter of rabbits? She'd have to find homes for them or take them to the animal shelter.

When she explained to Justin that she'd have to send a note home to his father, he brightened. "Are you going to have to see him again?"

Wanting to reassure him, she squeezed his shoulder. "I don't think so. You know the difference between right and wrong. I think we can work it out."

"Oh."

She saw the dejected droop of his shoulders. She was feeling pretty depressed herself. What kind of teacher did that make her if she couldn't help a troubled child? Maybe she was in the wrong profession after all.

"Are you very mad, Dad?" Justin asked.

Dave looked from the note to his son, whose lips trembled ever so slightly. "On a scale of one to ten, I'd say I'm an eleven."

"An eleven?"

Dave nodded grimly. "What're we gonna do, Justin? This isn't like you."

"I'm sorry, Dad." Small arms found their way around his neck.

Dave hugged his son back. It was difficult to tell who was doing the comforting. Reluctantly, he eased Justin away and looked at him. "Why? Why would you do something like that?"

"I can't tell you."

Whatever he'd expected, that wasn't it.

"You knew it was wrong."

"Yes."

"And you went ahead and did it anyway?"

Justin hung his head. "Yes, sir."

"I'm going to have to punish you."

"I know."

"Go on up to your room. I'll be up after a while."

Justin hated to see the disappointment in

34

his dad's eyes. It made him feel real sad inside. He knew his dad worked hard and didn't need more worry when he got home.

Miss McGuire had been disappointed too. Justin felt almost as bad about that as he did disappointing his dad. He brightened. That must mean they had something in common. Maybe this was the thing that would get them together.

He was prepared to take his punishment. Getting his dad and his teacher to see that they belonged together was worth it.

When his father knocked lightly, Justin called for him to come in. When he saw the disappointment that shadowed his father's eyes, he shifted his gaze away. "I guess you're going to have to call my teacher, huh?"

"I guess you're right."

"Do you think you ought to go see her?"

Something in his son's voice caught Dave's attention. "You sound like you want me to meet with Miss McGuire again."

"Gosh, no, Dad. No guy wants his dad to meet his teacher."

"Yeah," Dave said, and sighed. "What happened, Justin? You used to like school, and now it's one thing after another."

Justin shrugged. "Maybe I'm going through a phase."

Dave's lips twitched with the need to grin. A phase? Where had his son picked that up from? His smile faded. It had been four years since Marie had walked out on them. Had he failed to recognize that his son was having problems? Justin *seemed* happy enough, but lately, he'd been in a series of scrapes at school. Dave thought he'd been managing all right, but obviously he was missing something.

What was he going to do with his son? he asked himself, his frown deepening into a scowl. He'd thought they had things straightened out. Now Justin had gone and done something that even the most easygoing teacher — or parent — couldn't ignore.

What was he supposed to do? Should he look into counseling? If he went that route, where did he find the right person? Maybe Katie — Miss McGuire, he corrected himself — could suggest someone.

Feeling fractionally better, he wondered about a suitable punishment for Justin. He couldn't let this pass with just a father-son talk. He could take away Nintendo privileges for a week. Justin would consider that a fate worse than death.

Then again, maybe not. Justin had been preoccupied lately, spending long hours in his room. When Dave questioned him about it, Justin had said he'd been working on his Christmas list. A teasing comment that it was still pretty early to be thinking about Christmas only elicited a shrug, intriguing Dave more than ever.

He needed to get back on track, he reminded himself. Right now, he had a son who was waiting for his punishment.

"Dad, have you decided what you're gonna do?" Justin asked in a small voice.

Dave gave in to the need to take his son in his arms. He held Justin, this precious gift of life, close. As long as they were together, they could handle anything else. Even a pregnant rabbit, he thought, his sense of humor kicking in.

"What do you think I should do?"

Justin studied his sneakers.

"I don't know."

"No Nintendo for a week."

"Okay."

Justin's cheerful acceptance of the punishment had Dave more perplexed than ever.

That night, after Justin had gone to bed, Dave called the number on the note. "Miss McGuire, this is Dave Chase — Justin's father."

"I'm glad you called, Mr. Chase . . .

37

Dave." The sound of her husky voice temporarily distracted him from the purpose of the call.

"What can I do?"

"Justin is a normal little boy," she assured him. "He's testing his limits. Sometimes some extra attention at home goes a long way in helping a child feel secure."

Dave bristled and started to say that Justin received all the attention he needed, but something held him back. Obviously, something was bothering his son. It was up to him to find out what.

"Justin and I had a long talk tonight," he said. "I'm hoping that will help."

"I'm sure it will." Her voice, as velvety as a winter night, soothed away some of his weariness.

He spent a moment basking in it and the image it conjured up of her warm eyes and sympathetic smile. "I appreciate you taking the time to talk with me about him."

"Anytime. Justin's a special little boy. I want to do everything I can to help him."

"Thank you." He'd heard the hesitation in her voice. "Was there something more, Miss McGuire?"

"Don't let this thing with Justin get you discouraged. He's a wonderful little boy. Justin told me his mother died a few years back. I just wanted to say I know how hard it must be for you to raise him on your own."

"My wife's not dead," Dave said flatly.

"But — "

"She walked out on us four years ago." He hung up without saying good-bye.

A moment later, he regretted his rudeness. He didn't have to take out his temper on Justin's teacher. She'd only been expressing concern, and he'd all but bitten her head off. Katie McGuire sounded like she genuinely cared about Justin. That he'd been in the wrong didn't improve his temper any.

He'd thought he was over the bitterness, but he'd only been fooling himself. How long did it take to regain his faith in the basic goodness of people?

The dial tone buzzed in her ear.

Katie hung up the phone, smiling as she remembered Dave Chase's voice. Its deep, mellow tones had warmed her, and he'd sounded genuinely worried about his son. She'd touched a nerve when she mentioned his wife. His voice had hardened, flattened.

Now she tried to recall Justin's exact words. Too late, she remembered that a child didn't couch things in euphemisms.

39

When Justin had said his mother wasn't with them any longer, she'd taken that to mean she was dead. She'd never dreamed that his mother had left him.

How could a woman abandon her son? Especially a sensitive child like Justin. You had only to look in his eyes to see the curiosity, the sweet innocence of childhood.

Shaking her head at her musings, she settled back in bed, tucked her hair behind her ear, and picked up the education journal she'd been reading. The article she'd found so engrossing only minutes ago now failed to hold her interest.

For a moment . . . only a moment . . . she imagined herself going out with an attractive, sensitive man — a man with Dave Chase's features. A year had passed since she'd broken her engagement to Todd, a career-oriented stockbroker who had wanted her to give up her teaching job in order to be available to entertain his clients.

She'd realized that they wanted different things from life. Since then, she'd avoided relationships. Occasionally, however, she found herself wishing for someone to spend an evening with, someone she could share thoughts and feelings with. She flicked off the light and reminded herself that she liked her life just the way it was.

When the call came the following evening, she was cutting out construction paper pumpkins to decorate a bulletin board. She snatched up the phone and clamped it between her ear and her shoulder. "Hello."

"Miss McGuire, it's Dave Chase."

The voice was everything she'd remembered. Deep and warm — and worried. "Is something wrong with Justin?"

"No . . . that is, nothing's wrong with Justin. I wanted to apologize for how I acted last night. I didn't mean to snap at you. It's just . . ."

"That's all right," she said, wanting to save him any further embarrassment. "I misunderstood the situation."

"I appreciate what you've done for Justin. He talks about you all the time."

That surprised a chuckle from her. "And here I was afraid that I'd disgraced myself forever by keeping him in from recess."

"I don't think you have to worry about that." A pause stretched, lingered, as though he wanted to add more. "Well, that's all I wanted to say."

"Thanks for calling."

She held the receiver long after he'd hung up.

The next few days passed without problem. Apparently the talk Dave Chase had with Justin had had the desired effect.

"Miss McGuire, how long is four days?" Emilie asked.

Katie speared her fingers through her hair, pushing it back from her face. Halloween was only four days away. For her class of first-graders, it might as well be four months.

"Not very long," she said gently. "Remember how we said that hours make up a day?"

Emilie nodded.

"Well, there's twenty-four hours in a day. Four days would make ninety-six. So Halloween is just ninety-six hours away."

"Ninety-six." Emilie's lower lip drooped in dejection.

Too late, Katie realized she hadn't helped matters. "Halloween will be here sooner than you think. Sometimes, if you think about something else, what you're waiting for will come faster."

Emilie appeared to think about it. "I'll try."

Katie tousled the blond curls. "You do that."

"Mith McGuire knows what she's talking about," Justin said. "She's the smartest teacher in the school."

Two days before Halloween, she realized she'd been premature in thinking that whatever was prompting Justin's misbehavior had been solved. Following lunch, she found the pumpkin she'd carved for the class shattered, its insides spilled all over the floor.

His angelic appearance notwithstanding, Justin had single-handedly managed to turn her class into a circus in the last two weeks. She couldn't let this latest episode get by with only a missed recess as punishment.

This time her note asked for a meeting with Dave, suggesting they make it for tomorrow's parent-teacher conference.

Parent-teacher conferences were a teacher's nightmare. Trying to fit in thirty-two sets of parents with thirty-two different schedules into a two-day time frame demanded the balancing powers of a master juggler.

When Dave Chase showed up for his five-o'clock appointment, she felt some of the day's frustrations slip away. He was undoubtedly the best-looking man she'd seen in a long time.

She spent a few moments showing him Justin's work.

He looked at one picture and smiled, passing the paper back to her so that she could see what had captured his attention.

"My teacher," the caption read in childish printing. She didn't know whether to be flattered or not as she gazed at the portrait of her featuring yellow hair, a smile a yard wide, and skinny legs.

"Good likeness," Dave said, straight-faced.

"Mmm. I didn't know my arms were quite that long."

Their gazes returned to the picture, where rubbery-looking arms hung practically to the ground. As if on cue, they burst out laughing.

Sobering, Dave laid the picture aside. "Justin's got a good eye for a pretty lady."

The casually given compliment shouldn't have caused her to flush. Nevertheless, she could feel the color creeping into her cheeks.

"Uh . . . maybe we should talk about what's bothering him." She paused. "Justin said his mother left four years ago."

He heard the question in her voice. "He was just two when it happened. I don't know how much he remembers about her. He doesn't talk about her much."

You don't talk about her much, his conscience's voice reminded him.

"I'm sorry," she said quietly.

Though her voice was soft, he felt the sincerity of her words. "Thank you."

They spent the next ten minutes discussing various reasons behind Justin's behavior.

"I don't know what's gotten into him," Dave said, shaking his head.

"It's just not like him," Katie agreed. "He's active, like any other six-year-old, but he's never been deliberately naughty." She steepled her fingers together and rested her chin on them, drawing his attention to the dimple that made its home just to the right of her mouth. With a jolt, he realized he'd been focusing more on her than on his son's misbehavior. Bad idea.

It felt very much like a good idea, though. He pulled up short. The direction his thoughts had taken startled him. He had no intention of getting involved with Katie, no matter how charming he found her.

On the way home he felt more confused than ever. Justin seemed happy, so why was he acting up during the last month? Try as he would, Dave couldn't think of any event that could have triggered the series of mischievous acts at school.

"Dad, can you come to the Halloween party on Friday?" Justin asked that evening, sticking his finger into the peanut butter jar and carefully licking it clean.

Dave was about to reprimand him when he remembered how he'd done the same thing when he'd been six. His mother had looked the other way when he'd swiped a taste from the peanut butter jar.

"Can you, Dad?"

"I'll be there." It would mean rearranging an already complicated schedule, but he'd do that and more if it made Justin happy.

"We're supposed to wear costumes."

"We'll find you something."

"You need to wear one too."

"I don't think — "

"Mith McGuire said everybody's s'pposed to wear a costume."

"What's your teacher going as?" Dave asked casually.

"I dunno. She said it was a surprise."

Costume shopping for a six-year-old boy wasn't hard. They decked Justin out as a horned dinosaur with no problem. Finding a costume for a six-foot-two, one-hundred-and-eighty-pound man was far more difficult. Dave's mother came to the rescue with an orange-dyed sheet. Stuffed with cotton batting, he made a passable pumpkin.

"There," she said, sticking three leaves made from green felt into the neckline of the pumpkin suit. "I think it looks pretty good, if I do say so myself. Come look in the mirror."

He let her lead him to the mirror. His reflection nearly caused him to gag before his sense of humor took over.

"Thanks, Mom." He kept the smile from his voice as his gaze met hers in the mirror.

She looked equally grave. "You're welcome."

"You look good, Dad," Justin said between giggles.

"Yeah," his father seconded, a laugh rumbling from him. "Real good."

"I hope Mith McGuire likes pumpkins," Justin added.

Dave surprised himself by hoping the same thing.

Feeling more than a bit self-conscious, Dave walked through the school hallway until he came to the first grade classroom. Justin gave a squeal when he saw his father and bounded over to him.

"You came, Dad. You came."

"I promised I'd be here."

He endured the amused stares other parents directed at him and searched the room for Katie. When he saw her, his heartbeat picked up.

Schoolteachers never looked like that when he was a kid.

The ankle-length skirt with its rustling bustle and the lace-trimmed blouse were straight out of the last century. With her hair drawn up in a bun, she looked like an old-fashioned schoolmarm. A pair of half-glasses perched on her nose completed the image.

The costume suited her, emphasizing her femininity. Even the severe hairdo only added to her loveliness.

He knew when she saw him.

Biting her lip, Katie didn't smile, but she might as well have. It was there in her eyes, in the deepening of her dimple.

Dave shot her a sharp look that dared her to say anything.

"You make a . . . a great pumpkin," she said when she was sure her amusement was under control.

The darkening of his eyes promised retribution later. Her smile came out from under wraps as she thought about how much she liked him.

Like was too mild a word. A man who was willing to dress up like a pumpkin just to please his small son was a very special kind of man. It was at that moment that she admitted her feelings for Dave Chase went beyond physical attraction. Maybe it was his willingness to dress up as a giant pumpkin to please Justin. Maybe it was his determination to do the right thing for Justin, no matter what the cost to him.

She was beginning to see the man inside, and she liked him every bit as much as the appealing outer one. She let her gaze meet his. His eyes, the color of the sky just before dusk, were filled with laughter. His chip-toothed smile invited her to share his amusement. Even with the bulky pumpkin suit, he radiated self-confidence and vitality.

Breathing became difficult. She wet her lips and exhaled slowly, slipping a finger inside the collar of her costume, which suddenly seemed hot and stuffy.

Tension shimmered in the air, closing the distance between them, though neither moved. Katie stood rooted where she was, unable to go forward, unwilling to retreat. His gaze settled on her with unnerving thoroughness.

Intimacy. In the best sense of the word. It was there in the shared laughter that silently passed between them, in the meeting of their gazes. It made him think of all those old-fashioned words like closeness, caring, trust.

He felt a vise close around his heart even as he told himself it was nothing. He couldn't allow it to be anything. Not if he wanted to keep his heart intact.

Walk away, he told himself. The temptation was great to put distance between them, but greater still was the need to bask in the warmth that surrounded her. He wasn't the only one affected. Others seemed equally pulled to Katie, to the soft sound of her laughter, the quiet way she included everyone, children and parents alike, in the charmed circle that surrounded her.

He wanted her. And he didn't. No, that wasn't right. He couldn't. He couldn't want her and still keep himself and Justin safe from the hurt that came from caring.

Whatever happened between himself and Katie, he had to protect his son. That was the bottom line.

After making sure Justin was all right, he headed to the refreshment table to try the orange punch and jack-o'-lantern cookies he'd spotted earlier.

Katie watched as he made his escape.

Darn the man. First he looked at her as

though he couldn't get enough of her, and then he walked away without a backward glance.

"Miss McGuire?" Emilie pulled at her skirt. "Miss McGuire, will you tie my bow?"

Katie looked down at the small Raggedy Ann face with its exaggerated sprinkling of freckles and painted nose and cheeks. She tweaked one of the red yarn ponytails. "Turn around."

Obligingly, Emilie turned around, her white pinafore billowing out around lace-trimmed pantaloons. She did indeed look like one of the old-fashioned dolls.

Katie tied an extra-wide bow and then planted a kiss on Emilie's head. "There you go, sweetheart."

"Thank you," Emilie called, already scampering away.

There were other costumes to adjust, wigs to reattach, mustaches to draw. Caught up in the excitement, she didn't notice the small tug at her sleeve until it became more insistent.

"Mith McGuire." Justin, dressed as a horned dinosaur, held out a paper cup. "I brought you some punch."

The sweetness of his smile touched her heart, as it always did. "Thank you, Justin."

He beamed.

Emilie was at her side again, pulling at her skirt. "Miss McGuire, it's time for the parade."

"I'm coming," she said.

Emilie tugged harder. "Hurry. We're going to miss it."

Katie picked up her pace and tried to focus on the party. If Dave Chase wanted to give her one of his smoldering looks and then walk away, it was all right with her.

Sure it is, a sarcastic voice muttered. And if she believed that, she ought to look into buying some swampland in Florida.

Chapter Three

Sleep didn't come easily that night. Dave finally propped open a book and pretended to read, all the time thinking about Katie. Seeing her at the school party had triggered something inside him. It took him a while to identify the feeling.

When he did, he wanted to deny it. Truth was, he was lonely. Gut-deep lonely. The kind of loneliness that even the company of a much-loved son couldn't assuage. The kind of loneliness that craved a woman's company.

He'd felt that way once before. Giving in to the loneliness had resulted in making the worst mistake of his life.

He'd met Marie right after the business had started to take off. He'd been bowled over by her looks. She was the most beautiful woman he'd ever seen. That was no excuse for ignoring the warning signals. He'd been deaf to anything but Marie's beauty and how she made him feel.

The signs were there, if he'd cared to look — Marie's self-absorption, her preoccupation with how much he made, her insistence that they wait to start their family.

When she found she was pregnant just ten months after their marriage, she'd been furious. She'd blamed him. He could still hear her screams, the vile words she'd hurled at him. She withdrew from him.

Dave had hoped . . . prayed . . . that after the baby was born, she'd feel differently.

When Justin arrived a month early, she retreated from Dave even further. She hadn't wanted to take care of a baby, especially one who needed lots of extra care as Justin had.

He'd had to hire a nanny to stay with Justin because Marie had the habit of taking off to go shopping, out to lunch with friends, anywhere, as long as it wasn't at home.

When she said she wanted a divorce, he'd been relieved. Then came the deal. He'd cashed in his stock in the company and everything else he had.

He didn't regret the loss of the money. It had bought him custody of Justin. No, he didn't think a child could be bought. But peace of mind could. He had a paper that stated that Marie relinquished all claims to the child she'd given birth to but had never loved.

He'd pay twice that much and more to ensure that Justin remained with him. He didn't claim to be a perfect father; he had only one thing to offer. His love.

If he had a choice, he'd do it all over again. No father could ask for a more wonderful gift. Sometimes, though, he longed for someone to share his life with. Someone like . . .

His mind conjured up a picture of Katie.

It wouldn't hurt to ask her out. Intuitively, he knew he'd enjoy her company. As his mother had pointed out more than once, it was time to start dating again. And he couldn't think of anyone he'd rather spend time with than Katie.

When he called her that night to invite her to dinner, she sounded surprised. Well, what had he expected? He'd gone out of his way to keep their relationship at arm's length.

If she'd sounded surprised, he was even more so by her quick acceptance. He continued holding the receiver long after the dial tone buzzed in his ear. Her voice made him think of warm summer nights and ocean breezes.

You're losing it, man, he told himself with an involuntary glance outside. A cold, sleeting rain pelted the trees and bushes, and he was daydreaming like some moony-eyed teenager. He wondered if he remembered how to behave on a date.

A grin snuck up on him. If Katie could handle thirty-two six-year-olds, maybe she could deal with his social ineptness as well.

The next evening, he told his mother about the dinner and asked her to baby-sit.

"How's your credit?" she asked.

"My credit?"

"Is it good?"

"It's fine."

"Great. Because we're going shopping."

"Shopping?"

She grabbed her purse and pushed him to the door. "Come on. Your dad can watch Justin while we go to the mall."

"I thought you had a book club meeting."

"I did, but this is more important." Her gaze flicked over him. "You look like a refugee from a nerd convention."

He started to bristle at the insult, but she was already hurrying to the car.

"Mom," he said, catching up with her, "I can buy my own clothes. And what's wrong with what I have on?"

She rolled her eyes. "You really do need help."

Two hours later, Dave found himself with a half dozen shirts in a rainbow of colors, a couple of pairs of jeans and chinos, gray dress slacks, and a navy blazer.

"They're too tight," he protested at the jeans.

"Nonsense. They're just right. Women like a nice tush."

"Mom!"

"Stop thinking like an uptight father and start thinking like a man who's out to find himself a woman."

Dave sighed, preparing himself for the "you're-too-young-to-stay-single-for-the-rest-of-your-life" lecture. His mother had been encouraging him to start dating for the last couple of years.

"Justin says she's pretty," she said unexpectedly.

A picture of Katie McGuire appeared in his mind. She was more than pretty, he decided, with her soft hair framing a heart-shaped face. Her lips were a shade too full, just right for kissing.

Still, he felt bound to protest. He didn't want his mother getting the wrong idea. "I'm not looking — "

"Save it. If you're not, it's time you started." More gently, she added, "Marie's been gone four years. How long do you intend to punish yourself for falling for her?"

"I'm not . . ."

"Aren't you? Isn't that why you've refused to go out and enjoy yourself? Because you think you don't deserve to be happy."

Silently, he acknowledged the truth of her words. It was more than that, though. He was scared. Scared of caring again and possibly making the same mistake. Scared of introducing another woman into his son's life and having her take off. He hadn't been able to prevent what happened with Marie, but he didn't intend to make the same mistake again.

"It won't hurt to test the waters," his mother said, picking up the conversation. "Who knows, she may like engineers who wear pocket protectors."

He thought about her words that night after he'd cleaned up the kitchen and tucked Justin in bed.

Trying to be both mother and father to a six-year-old boy and running his own software firm didn't leave much spare time or energy for anything else. The excuses fell flat, though, as he acknowledged the real reason he'd avoided involvement.

He was afraid. It wasn't the idea of dating. It was Katie herself. He sensed that she could become important to him.

Self-consciously, he dressed in the new slacks, shirt, and blazer the following evening.

When his mother arrived to baby-sit, she gave him an approving look. "Now you don't look like an engineer."

"Since when is looking like an engineer bad?"

"Since you're seeing a pretty woman."

"I'm not seeing — "

"You're not seeing who?" Justin asked.

"Whom," Dave and his mother corrected together.

"Whom," Justin repeated patiently.

"Your father's seeing Miss McGuire."

"I'm not seeing — "

"Wow! Really, Dad?"

Dave threw his son a sharp look. Something was going on here, and he was determined to find out what.

Before he could pursue it, his mother all but pushed him out the door. "Don't hurry home. We'll be fine."

Katie's home was an old brownstone house divided into apartments. Following her directions, he climbed the stairs to the top floor.

"Come in," a voice called after he rang the bell.

Shaking his head — after all, he could've been anyone — he let himself in.

"I'll be out in a minute," she said from another room.

He took his time to look around. High ceilings and stained-glass windows gave evidence to the house's age while brightly colored posters and plants added a contemporary touch. The furnishings owed more to whimsy and imagination than to money. The overall effect was one of warmth, an invitation to make oneself at home.

He thought of his own house, furnished to accommodate a bachelor and a small boy. Though it was comfortable enough, it lacked the homey air Katie's small apartment had. It needed a woman's touch, his mother had told him more than once. He'd ignored that, but now he had a feeling she might be right.

"Sorry to keep you waiting," Katie said, appearing in the doorway of what he assumed to be the bedroom.

Dave reminded himself that this was Justin's teacher, but seeing her in a soft peach sweater and skirt that gently clung to her curves made it hard to remember. "You look great." She looked more than great.

If he hadn't been so bowled over by her superficial resemblance to Marie at their first meeting, he'd have realized she was far more lovely than his ex-wife. Her looks weren't as obvious; her beauty radiated from an inner glow that spilled over in the brightness in her eyes, the warmth of her smile.

"So do you." Flags of color stained her cheeks.

He found himself unexpectedly charmed. Katie might resemble his ex-wife in looks, but her shyness was a refreshing contrast. His lips tightened as he recalled Marie's calculated methods of getting what she wanted.

He wasn't going to fall into that trap again. Katie was nothing like Marie.

"You ought to keep your door locked," he said once they were outside. He cupped her elbow to help her over the rough clumps of grass that served as a front yard.

"You sound like my ex-fiancé." She didn't make it sound like a compliment. "He was always telling me I was inviting trouble."

"He had a point," he said as he opened the car door for her.

"Maybe. I prefer to think the best about people. So far no one's robbed me, unless you count my neighbor who borrows a cup of sugar every week and always forgets to replace it."

A wry grin skimmed his lips as he realized he wasn't going to change her thinking. What's more, he realized he didn't *want* to. He liked her just the way she was.

She kept him entertained during dinner with stories about her first-graders. Beneath the laughter, he heard the affection and genuine love. He tried to imagine teaching thirty-two six-year-olds for seven hours a day five days a week . . . and failed.

When he said as much, she chuckled. "You get used to it."

He loved the way laughter brightened her eyes and softened her mouth, suffusing her whole face with joy.

"You really like what you're doing, don't you?"

"Of course not. I got into teaching because of the big bucks."

He laughed. "Point taken."

"How about you? Do you like what you're doing?"

He thought about it. Owning a software firm had been his dream for as long as he could remember. Lately, though, it had lost much of its excitement. More accurately, he'd lost his enthusiasm for the job. Maybe because he had no one to share the triumphs and the failures with. When he'd married Marie, he'd thought he'd found that someone.

He'd been wrong.

Aware that she was waiting for an answer, he nodded. "Yeah. I like it."

"Do I hear a but in there somewhere?"

Her perception caught him unprepared. How had she sensed what he was only beginning to understand? "How'd you know?"

She lifted one shoulder. "Something in your voice, like you weren't sure."

"Designing software's what I always wanted to do," he said slowly.

"But . . ." she prompted.

"Once the business took off, I had to stop designing and start managing. Seems like all I do now is sign papers and keep the phone glued to my ear." Voicing his thoughts aloud startled him. It was the first time he'd admitted to his dissatisfaction. He didn't much like the feeling that she'd so quickly seen what he hadn't been aware of himself until lately.

"How'd you do that?" he asked.

"Do what?"

"Figure out that something was bothering me about work."

The dimple at the side of her mouth

deepened. "I didn't do anything except ask questions. You did the rest."

He wasn't so sure about that. The warm interest in her eyes invited sharing. He found himself very much wanting to do just that.

Before he knew what he was doing, he told her about the early days, about trying to start up a business with nothing more than a dream and a couple of thousand dollars he'd borrowed from the bank.

There'd been lean years, years he wasn't sure he was going to make it. What he'd lacked in business know-how, he'd made up for in energy and vision. Looking at the woman sitting across from him, he had a feeling she'd understand the need that had driven him to make his dream come true.

She didn't say much. She seemed content to listen. The questions she did ask, though, showed a grasp of software design that surprised him.

"You sound like you know what you're talking about. Have you ever designed software?"

"I did. Once."

"What made you quit?"

She was silent for a long time, and he wondered if she was going to answer his question. "I wanted to make a difference."

"That's why you chose teaching?"

"I always liked kids. When I was little, I wished I'd grown up in a big family. So I went back to school and got my elementary ed degree." She smiled. "Sounds pretty corny, doesn't it?"

He shook his head. "Sounds pretty wonderful."

"Don't make me out to be some kind of a martyr. Working with the kids . . . it's the greatest." A flush worked its way into her cheeks as if she were embarrassed by the admission. "I love what I do."

He saw the sparkle in her eyes. "It shows." He leaned across the table, intent on kissing her, before he realized what he'd been about to do. Instead, he skimmed her jaw with the tip of his thumb. The touch wasn't enough, and he laid his palm against her cheek, absorbing the shape, the texture of it. With more control than he knew he possessed, he dropped his hand.

He took her home soon after that, more intrigued than ever. The lady was a fascinating blend of sophistication and naïveté, shrewdness and idealism. He didn't know where they were heading. All he knew for sure was that he very much wanted to see her again.

Even the grilling his mother subjected

him to couldn't dampen his enthusiasm.

"Enough, Mom," he said when she asked him when he was going to ask Katie out again.

The memory of that almost-kiss remained with him far into the night, puzzling him, scaring him. Most of all, he wondered about Katie's reaction if he'd given in to the need to touch his lips to hers. Would she have welcomed it or turned away?

He'd been going to kiss her, Katie thought as she got ready for bed. She knew it, had seen it in his eyes, had heard it in the hitch of his breath as he'd leaned toward her, had felt it in the tenderness of his touch when he'd stroked her cheek. The kiss had been but a heartbeat away, but he hadn't followed through.

Something had held him back. She didn't know whether she was relieved or disappointed. A little bit of both, probably. A kiss would take their relationship to a new level, something she wasn't sure she was ready for.

She wondered what his lips would taste like, what it would be like to be held by him. Instinctively, she knew he would be gentle. He wasn't a man to use his strength against a woman.

That night when she fell asleep, she dreamed about Prince Charming — a Prince Charming with Dave Chase's face.

The strong light of morning and a cup of coffee had her feeling foolish. She'd dated the man exactly once, and already she was dreaming about him.

Obviously, she needed to get out more if one date had her acting like a lovesick teenager mooning over the captain of the football team.

"Did you and my dad have a good time?" Justin asked when he helped her pass out papers before school began.

He'd started arriving a few minutes early, always eager to help. After checking with Dave that it was all right, she'd put him to work. Their conversations usually consisted of Justin asking about her likes and dislikes. More than once, she'd had the feeling that his questions had a deeper meaning than what appeared on the surface.

Today's question took her by surprise. Being quizzed about a date by a first-grader wasn't something she was accustomed to.

"Did you?" he persisted.

"A real good time."

"Are you gonna go out with him again?"

Maybe he was concerned that she'd come between him and his father. "Would you mind?" she asked gently.

"Gosh, no."

"Then why all the questions?"

"No reason. I just wanted to know." He went on to extol his father's virtues and talents. "Dad can do 'most anything."

He took off after that, and she was left to wonder why she felt that she'd just been grilled by an expert.

Thoughts of Dave kept intruding upon her thoughts, distracting her to the point that she'd passed out two sets of the same assignment.

When Emilie Taylor whispered her mistake to her, Katie flushed and quickly gathered up the extra papers. She happened to catch Justin watching her.

When the phone rang that night, she grabbed for it.

"Katie, it's Dave. I enjoyed last night." A smile sounded in his voice.

"So did I."

"Maybe we could do it again. Does Friday night sound all right?"

It sounded wonderful. He named a restaurant on the outskirts of town, a fairly new one with a reputation for exotic fare.

"Uh-uh," she said. "This time dinner's on me. How does homemade spaghetti sound?"

"Great. May I bring something?"

"Just yourself."

She was smiling when she hung up the phone. Smiling and anticipating Friday night.

A home-cooked meal wasn't a novelty to him. His mother invited Justin and him to dinner on a regular basis; besides, his own cooking wasn't half bad. But having dinner opposite a beautiful woman in her apartment had a whole different appeal.

He liked the way she didn't apologize for the school papers scattered across the sofa and coffee table. He liked how she invited him right into the kitchen while she cooked. Come to think of it, there wasn't much he didn't like about Katie.

While she cooked, he took his time looking at her. Tiny ceramic apples adorned her ears. She'd left her hair unbound, held back by a narrow red ribbon. Pristine white jeans showed off a spectacular pair of legs and a tiny waist. With them, she wore a red sweater, loose and casual. Her face was scrubbed clean, making her look nearly as young as the high school girl he occasionally hired to baby-sit Justin.

The overall effect was one of wholesome freshness. And very appealing.

"I hope you're hungry," she said. "I made lots."

The food was hearty without being heavy. Spaghetti with homemade sauce and a tossed salad didn't exactly qualify as gourmet fare, but it was by far the best meal he'd had in a long time. *Admit it, man,* he thought in a burst of honesty. *I wouldn't care if I was eating sawdust.*

It was Katie who transformed a simple meal into a special one, Katie who brightened what should have been an ordinary evening into something extraordinary, Katie who made him start thinking of soft moonlit nights and winter evenings in front of a fireplace.

"Anything wrong?" she asked.

He hadn't time to respond when she laid a small hand on his. Her touch, whisper soft, pushed him up and out of his seat. Before she could react, he fitted a finger beneath her chin and tilted her chin up. When he lowered his head to meet her lips, he forgot all the reasons he shouldn't kiss her, forgot all his strictures against involvement, and simply felt.

Her lips were soft and tasted of spaghetti

sauce. The combination shouldn't have been so appealing, but it was. Then again, with Katie, nothing was as it should be.

A woman who looked like her should be spending the evening in an upscale restaurant, seeing and being seen. Admired. Instead, she was content to spend the time with him. Alone.

He deepened the kiss until he wasn't sure he remembered how to breathe. When he lifted his head, he drew a shaky breath.

"You taste . . ."

"Like spaghetti?"

"Incredible."

The coy comment he half expected didn't come. Instead, a tiny smile played across her lips.

"Wait until you taste dessert."

Even the dessert, which she called "death by chocolate," failed to wipe away the memory of the kiss.

"How'd you know chocolate's my favorite?" he asked, spooning another bite of the decadently rich cake to his lips.

Her smile became wider. "Justin told me." She cut him a second piece.

He ignored his mother's warnings about cholesterol levels and savored each bite. "You could bottle this stuff and make a fortune."

"It'd be hard to eat out of a bottle."

"You're right. Don't bottle it." He finished off the last bite.

She didn't clear away the dishes but left them where they were. He liked that she wasn't hung up on appearances, either with herself or her home. Her casual acceptance of papers on the sofa and dishes on the table made him feel at home in a way nothing else could have.

She made hot chocolate and carried it into the living room. The homey act warmed him even before he sipped the rich brew from the mug she handed him. She'd added marshmallows to the chocolate, something he hadn't had since he'd been somewhere around Justin's age.

He couldn't remember the last time he'd spent an evening just talking. That he was talking with a beautiful woman was an added bonus. But, as attractive as Katie was, that wasn't what drew him to her.

It was her warmth, her genuine interest in what he was saying, that had him opening up as he'd never done before. To his surprise, he found himself telling her about Marie.

"Did you love her?"

He'd thought he was in love with her, of course, or he would never have married her. But that love had quickly died when her true colors revealed themselves. The pain he'd suffered when she'd left was more a loss of a dream than for Marie herself.

Aware that he hadn't answered Katie, he smiled faintly. "I thought so. Once."

To his relief, she didn't ask what had happened. She simply laid her hand on his and squeezed gently. "I'm sorry."

"Thanks." He hadn't expected to say what he said next. But nothing that had happened so far with Katie was as he'd planned. "You look like her."

He felt her slight start, the subtle withdrawal. What had he been thinking of, telling her that?

"That's why you were staring at me that day in the park?"

He nodded. "At first . . . I thought it was Marie. Except that she'd never be caught dead jogging in a city park."

"She didn't like to exercise?"

"Only in a health club."

"And now? Do I still remind you of her?"

"Not anymore."

"Why not?"

He gave in to the impulse to pull her into his arms. After a slight hesitation, she relaxed against him. His arms tightened around her.

"You didn't answer my question," she reminded him quietly.

He didn't know how to explain what had set her apart from Marie. The physical differences were easy to catalog. Katie's eyes shone with an inner peace, while Marie's always reflected the discontent she felt with herself and everything around her. Katie's lips were full and generous, hinting at her unselfishness. Marie's mouth had a pinched look to it.

He could go on, but he knew Katie wouldn't be satisfied with that kind of superficial answer. "You know how to love. Marie never learned how to love anyone but herself."

The color that flooded her cheeks was but one more testament to the contrast between Katie and his ex-wife. He whispered a kiss across her lips. She returned it with shy hesitancy. "I . . . you . . . do you want some more hot chocolate?"

"Where do we go from here?" she asked after she'd refilled their cups.

The simple honesty of the question shook him. Here was a woman who didn't play games.

"I don't know." Honesty required honesty. Right now, it was all he could give. "I like you — I like you a lot. Maybe we could see where it takes us?" His breath lodged in his throat as he waited for her answer.

"I'd like that."

It seemed so easy, so natural, to take her in his arms. With her head tucked against his shoulder, she felt small and fragile. She was so full of energy, so vital, that he forgot just how tiny she really was.

He traced the delicate bones of her shoulders before sliding his hands down her arms to take her hands in his. He brought one hand to his lips and pressed a kiss to her palm.

"That's so you won't forget me."

She raised her lips to his. The kiss was like her — sweet and giving. "That's so you won't forget *me*."

There was no danger of that, he thought on his way home. No danger at all.

Chapter Four

Katie blew her bangs from her forehead. Another pair of hands would come in handy right about now. Helping thirty-two first-graders make a construction paper turkey was at least a two-person task. Unfortunately, her teaching aide had called in sick, leaving Katie to manage alone.

"Miss McGuire, my turkey looks geeky," Tyler complained.

She took a look at the lopsided turkey. The legs and feet extended from his neck while the feathers drooped from the belly. "Maybe if we change these around," she suggested, switching the legs with the feathers.

The poor fowl still resembled something from another universe, but it satisfied Tyler, who favored her with a toothless smile. "Thanks, teacher."

"You're welcome."

By the time the class finished the project, the floor was littered with scraps of colored paper and her blouse sported several spots of glue. Good thing she'd given up dry-clean-only clothes a long time ago.

As part of the Thanksgiving unit, the children were also drawing pictures of things they were thankful for. She strolled by the desks, looking at the various pictures — food, bicycles, pets. When she came to Justin's desk, she paused.

His picture showed a large man and a small boy. That wasn't surprising. He was obviously drawing his family.

"Is that you and your dad?" she asked.

He nodded. "Someday we're gonna have a mom too."

She swallowed hard. "I know you will, sweetheart."

"She won't leave like my other mom did. I'll be real good and not make her mad."

"Justin, your mother didn't leave because of anything you did. Parents don't leave their children because they get mad."

He shook his head. "Sammy Jackson said his dad left because Sammy left his bike in the driveway and his dad drove over it."

Words rushed to her lips. She was aware of Sammy's situation and knew his parents had a lot of problems, problems that had nothing to do with a crumpled bike. She'd have to talk with him about it, try to explain what to a child must seem incomprehensible.

Right now, though, Justin needed her.

She picked her way carefully through the morass of misconceptions and hurt. "Your mom and dad decided they couldn't live together anymore. It didn't have anything to do with you. Okay?"

He looked unconvinced but gave her a sweet smile that had her own lips curving upward. "Okay."

When she found Dave waiting for her at the end of the day, she couldn't help the pleasure that warmed her all over. Having him drop in unexpectedly was one of the nicest things about living in a small town. His office was only two blocks away.

"You're working late," he said, helping her on with her coat.

"Part of the job."

"Did you walk today?"

She nodded.

"How 'bout a ride home?"

His smile did funny things to her insides. When they reached her apartment, she invited him in. She'd made a batch of chocolate chip cookies the night before and set them on a plate before pouring two glasses of milk.

"Milk and cookies. Makes me feel about as old as Justin," Dave said wryly.

With his hair mussed by the wind and cheeks reddened by the cold, he looked very much like his son, she thought, and experienced the same fluttering in her stomach she'd felt when he kissed her.

Apparently he was remembering the same thing, for he lowered his head and took her mouth gently, so very gently. Her heart hammered and her breath hitched in her throat when he kissed her again.

She slipped her arms around his waist, feeling the play of muscles across his back. He was a big man, a strong man, a man who had gone his own way for a long time. Could he learn to accept a woman as part of his life?

The thought had her drawing back. She needed time to think, time to understand her needs before she could understand his. And then there was Justin.

Remembering her conversation with him today had her frowning.

"What's wrong?" Dave asked.

Should she tell him? Or would it only hurt him? If she were in his place, she'd want to know.

Quietly she told him about her talk with Justin.

Dave went very still, his shoulders tense, his hands clenched.

"Have you talked with Justin about Marie . . . why she left?"

"In a general sort of way," he said somewhat warily. "I think I explained it ade-quately."

"Are you sure about that?"

"Of course I'm sure. And anyway, Justin was barely more than a baby when she left. He doesn't even remember her."

"Children — even very young children — remember a lot more than we give them credit for."

"I know my own son."

She laid a hand on his arm. "I know it's hard to accept, but maybe Justin needs to talk about her. He needs to know the truth about why she left. I'm not an expert on child psychology, but I do know when a child's hurting. He needs you, Dave."

"He's got me."

"He needs you to trust him enough to talk with him, to tell him why he doesn't have a mother like the rest of the kids."

"He doesn't have a mother because she's a selfish, vindictive . . ."

"Did it ever occur to you that Justin might blame himself for her leaving? All he knows is that his mother left him. It's only natural that he'd want to know why."

"And you think he's blaming himself?" The idea clearly startled him.

"I think it's a possibility. Children get things twisted around sometimes, blaming themselves for what the adults in their lives do. I think Justin needs you to tell him what really happened. As much as he can understand."

"He doesn't need to know that his mother walked out on us because she couldn't bear the thought of being a mother."

The harshness of his voice saddened her, but she held her ground. "Have you asked him?"

"I don't need to."

"Maybe you ought to start thinking about what Justin needs."

"I've spent the last six years thinking about little else." The bleakness in his voice betrayed his pain.

"No one's doubting your love for your son."

"Yeah? You could've fooled me."

"If you'd only talk with him . . . explain to him that it wasn't his fault — "

"Of course it wasn't his fault. It was that selfish . . ." He shook his head. "I'll decide what's right for my son."

"Okay. Do something for me?" Without giving him time to answer, she said, "Ask yourself who you're trying to protect. Yourself or Justin."

Anger coiled within him at the accusation. Of course he was trying to protect his son. What father wouldn't?

"Why don't you mind your own business?" He regretted the words as soon as they were out. Katie had proved over and over that she cared about Justin, about all her students. He saw the pain shimmer in her eyes, then etch itself around her lips. He couldn't let that blind him to what was best for his son.

Stung, she felt her eyes fill with tears. Okay, so she wasn't Justin's parent, and maybe Dave's relationship with his son wasn't her business. That didn't mean she didn't know something about children. She'd been teaching for the last five years and had more than a little experience in dealing with kids, including children of divorced parents. Sometimes they internalized the problems of their parents, taking on a burden of guilt no child should be called upon to shoulder.

What she felt must have come through in her eyes, for Dave started to reach for her.

She swiped at the tears. Why couldn't he accept that she was only thinking of Justin? Dave seemed determined to believe the worst about her, no matter what she did.

For the first time she let herself question the wisdom of what she felt for him. If he couldn't get over his hang-up about her resemblance to his ex-wife, then there was no chance for them.

"Thanks for the snack," he said shortly, and let himself out.

The air had a snap to it, autumn's overture to winter. He walked three blocks before remembering his car. By the time he returned to get it, there was a parking ticket stuck on the windshield. Too late, he remembered he'd parked in a thirty-minute zone.

Katie had him going in circles. If he spent a little more time remembering Marie — and the pain she'd put him and Justin through — he'd probably put Katie out of his mind, Dave told himself grimly. He didn't need a woman in his life right now. Especially a nosy one who thought she knew more about raising his son than he did.

The idea that Justin might blame himself for Marie leaving them was so ridiculous that Dave wanted to laugh it away. The only problem was that the last thing he felt like doing was laughing.

Katie was a great teacher, but she didn't know what she was talking about. Justin barely remembered his mother. How could he feel guilty over her desertion? Even as he asked himself the question, he wondered. Was she right? Was Justin blaming himself?

With the self-discipline that had enabled him to survive the last four years, he shoved the questions from his mind. Maybe he didn't have a degree in teaching or child psychology, but he knew what was best for his son.

That took him full circle, back to Katie. He found he couldn't push her out of his mind as he'd done with Marie. Katie, with her gentle smile and warm eyes, was fixed there.

What frightened him the most was the fact that she felt something for him too. He could see it in her eyes, hear it in her voice. He couldn't allow what he felt for her — or she for him — to govern his actions.

He had a son who needed attention and a business that required more hours than he had to give. All his carefully marshaled arguments for avoiding a relationship with Katie, though, failed to erase the memory of the taste of her lips or the feel of her in his arms.

His mood hadn't improved any when he arrived at his parents' house to pick up Justin.

"You're about as much fun as a bear with an impacted wisdom tooth," his mother said mildly when he snapped at Justin to hurry up and get his coat on.

"Sorry," Dave said. "I've . . . got a lot on my mind."

"Like a certain pretty schoolteacher?"

"Leave Katie out of it."

"Oh, I'm willing to leave her out of it. I just wonder if you are."

With that cryptic statement, she kissed his cheek and headed back to the kitchen.

First Katie. And now his mother. What was with all the females in his life? Had they all gone crazy? Maybe the cold had cast a spell over them. Or maybe they'd succumbed to a malady that affected only women.

Neither explanation gave him any satisfaction, and he stomped out the door, only to remember that his son wasn't with him.

The twinkle in his mother's eyes as she and Justin waited at the door only served to increase his irritation.

"Dad?" Justin said on their way home.

"What?"

"Are you mad at me?"

The hesitant tone in his son's voice had Dave tightening his hands on the steering wheel. "Of course not. You're my best buddy, remember?"

"You look like you're mad. Like after Mom left."

Justin's words gave him pause. He hadn't thought that his son remembered much of that time when Marie had walked out on them. Obviously, he was wrong.

Did he look angry? He chose his words with care. "I'm sorry. I guess I am sort of mad. But not at you."

"Are you mad at Mith McGuire?"

"No."

"Then who?"

"Whom."

"That's what I said. Who're you mad at?"

"Me."

"You're mad at you?"

"Sounds pretty crazy, doesn't it?"

"Yeah," Justin said frankly. "How do you get mad at yourself?"

Dave spent the rest of the evening asking himself that same question.

During her lunch break, Katie received a message over the intercom that she had a telephone call. Puzzled, she hurried to the office. No one ever called her at school.

"Katie McGuire here."

"Ms. McGuire, this is Sally Chase — Justin's grandmother."

"Oh, yes, Mrs. Chase."

"I've got a little problem, dear, and hoped you could help me. Dave just called to say he has to stay late at work. Ordinarily, it wouldn't be a problem, but tonight's our bridge night. I'd cancel, but we're partners with another couple.

"I hate to ask, dear, but Justin talks about you all the time and I thought — "

"I'd love to stay with him, Mrs. Chase."

"You're sure it's not an imposition?"

"I'm sure," she said, ignoring her misgivings over accepting. The last time she'd seen Dave had left him angry and her frustrated. "I'll bring him home and stay with him until Dave . . . his father gets there."

"Thank you, dear. You're a lifesaver."

When she told Justin, he grabbed her around the legs, nearly toppling her over. "You're gonna stay at my house?" At her nod, he shouted, "Cool. Can we go right now?"

She leaned down to whisper conspiratorially, "Maybe we ought to wait till school lets out."

"Oh. Yeah." He lowered his voice to match hers. "I won't tell the other kids. They might get jealous or something."

"Or something."

After school, they stopped at a pizza place and ordered one-with-the-works to go and a six-pack of pop. At home, Justin put down four pieces before declaring he was full. He helped her clean up, chattering all the time. Only when she asked about his mother did he become silent.

"Dad doesn't want me to talk about her," he said at last.

A slight frown wrinkled her brow as she thought about the implications of his innocent words. Whether Dave knew it or not, Justin needed to talk about his mother. He needed to know it wasn't his fault that she'd left.

She started to remember the pictures she'd seen scattered through the living room and hanging in the hallway. There were plenty of Justin, a few of Dave, and several of an older couple, probably Dave's parents. But none of Justin's mother. It was as if she didn't exist, had never existed.

Katie wasn't allowed to dwell on it as Justin challenged her to a Nintendo duel. They played for an hour, with Justin the undisputed winner.

"Bedtime," she said when he rubbed his eyes. "We'll have a rematch another time."

"One more game. Maybe you'll win this one," he wheedled.

"One more," she agreed, knowing she

was being manipulated and not caring.

With Justin still the winner, they turned off the game and headed upstairs.

She took a look at his hands and face. "Bath first." She opened a door and found a brightly tiled bathroom.

"That's mine," he said, pointing to a duck-shaped soap. "Dad always gives me my bath with it."

By the time she bathed him and shampooed his hair, she was nearly as wet as he was.

"Hey, Mith McGuire, you're all wet," Justin said as she lifted him out of the tub.

She pulled a face. "I wonder how that happened."

"Maybe when you had to find the soap when I dropped it," he said helpfully.

She bundled his bath-flushed body into a towel and patted him dry. Unable to resist the just-washed smell of small boy, she hugged him to her.

He hugged her back. "I love you, Mith McGuire."

"Me too, honey," she whispered. "Me too." She'd give anything to make him her own. But she was astute enough to realize that it wasn't just the child she wanted. And honest enough to admit it.

"Mith McGuire, I'm cold," Justin said as

she continued to hold him. "I need my 'jamas."

Dismayed, she looked down to see goose bumps puckering his skin. She managed to find the right pair of pajamas — ones with dinosaurs sprinkled all over them — and get him into them. The homey acts of getting him ready for bed filled an empty place in her heart. Tears squeezed out of the corners of her eyes. She dabbed at them before he could notice. How could she expect a child to understand tears she couldn't explain to herself?

"I'll turn down your bed while you brush your teeth."

He gave her a pained look and placed small hands on his hips. "Do I hafta? I brushed them this morning."

She fisted her hands on her hips in like fashion. "Yes, you hafta." Ignoring his frown, she patted his dinosaur-clad bottom and watched as he trudged to the bathroom, only to be back within seconds.

"Did you brush?"

He nodded vigorously, his lips pinched together, before a laugh bubbled out.

Her heart turned to butter at the impish expression in his eyes.

She spotted a rocking chair with a worn cushion propped in it and sat down. "Does your dad rock you to sleep?"

He nodded. "Dad always reads to me before I go to sleep." He jumped off to run to shelves jammed with books and came back with a well-used copy of *Peter Pan*. He climbed into her lap. "Okay, I'm ready."

She was soon caught up in the familiar tale.

"Do it like my dad does," Justin said.

"How's your dad do it?"

"Like this." He gave a little-boy imitation of the pirate voice of Captain Hook.

"Oh." Her own impersonation of the pirate captain sent him into a fit of giggles. "Okay, buster, no laughing at my Captain Hook." With great aplomb, she assumed the voices of Peter, the Lost Boys, and Tinker Bell. Each sent him into another attack of giggles.

By now she was laughing as hard as he was. Laughing gave way to tickles.

"Okay, you," she said, pulling him back to her lap. "We've got a story to finish."

She resumed the story, assuming a stern expression when Justin threatened to dissolve in laughter again. Halfway through the book, he clamped a hand to his mouth, too late to stop a yawn.

Book forgotten, she began to rock him. The soothing rhythm had the desired effect. Soon Justin was snoring softly, his head nestled against her. Rather than move him, she continued to hold him, savoring the sweet scent of childhood and innocence. Love, a palpable force, thrummed through her as he snuggled more deeply into her arms.

What she felt for the son was simple and uncomplicated compared to what she felt for the father. And what did he feel for her? Had she imagined the occasional flashes of tenderness, the longing for something more than a few dates together?

She didn't think she had, but just as she thought they were making progress, Dave threw up a new set of barriers.

Chapter Five

It had been one of those days. Everything that could go wrong had chosen today to do so. With more than a little relief, Dave shook off the worries and let the feeling of home envelop him.

He wasn't sure how he felt about Katie pinch-hitting with Justin. When his mother had called to tell him she'd asked Katie to take Justin home from school and stay with him, Dave had been wary. He didn't want Katie reading any more into the request than there was. His relationship with her didn't include Justin. He didn't *want* it to include his son. It was a knee-jerk reaction that he knew was irrational; he knew it and didn't care.

When he didn't find her in the living room, he headed into the kitchen to let her know he was home. She wasn't there; neither did she answer his call. A little concerned, he took the stairs two at a time.

He hadn't known what he'd find. What he didn't expect was to see her asleep in the old rocking chair with Justin sprawled across her, his fist tangled in her hair, the book she must have been reading to him lying facedown on the floor.

Coming to a halt in the doorway, Dave felt his heart turn over. Telling himself it was nothing, he nevertheless took a moment to study the two of them. To the best of his knowledge, Marie had never read a bedtime story to their son. She'd been too afraid of having her clothes wrinkled or her hair mussed by sticky fingers.

Katie apparently had no such fears. She looked completely relaxed and totally comfortable with Justin cuddled in her arms.

Justin had never known what it was like to have a mother's arms around him as he snuggled against her to be rocked to sleep or to soothe away his nightmares. He hadn't known what he was missing.

Until now.

They looked like they belonged together, their gold-brown hair close enough in color that they could pass for mother and son.

Dave wasn't at all sure how he felt about that. Justin had a child's openness and honesty. He gave his heart with trusting faith. Hadn't Dave listened to his son's prayers where he'd asked God to bless Katie along with Daddy, Grandma, and Grandpa? The more Katie became involved in Justin's life, the more he'd expect her to be there. Always.

Always wasn't a word Dave was prepared to deal with. He didn't believe in it. Justin was too young to understand that there was no such thing in the real world. And Dave didn't want him learning that lesson any time soon. Life would teach it to him soon enough.

Justin shifted slightly as he searched for his thumb, a habit he'd outgrown except when he slept. With care not to wake Katie, Dave eased him from her arms. Justin, dead to the world once asleep, didn't stir as Dave picked him up and put him to bed.

Dave knew better than to stay, but he couldn't tear his eyes away from Katie. He was fascinated by the way her hair shone in the muted light of dusk, by the sweep of lashes that shadowed the soft curve of her cheek.

His gaze lowered to her slightly parted lips. They were soft and vulnerable looking, like Justin's. And yet not like his at all. Hers had the full ripeness of a woman's.

If only he hadn't kissed her, but he had. And he remembered. He remembered too well.

Her hands lay curled in her lap. He wanted to take one and press a kiss to the center of the soft palm. A honey-colored strand of hair tickled her cheek, and he eased it away. She stirred at his touch. When she settled with a sigh, he realized he'd been holding his breath. Slowly, deliberately, he pushed the air from his lungs.

He tucked an afghan around her, and, unable to help himself, brushed a kiss over her forehead. She murmured something before settling further into the chair. He ought to wake her, or at least move her. She'd be lucky if she didn't wake up with a stiff neck.

But he let her sleep. He liked seeing her here . . . in his home. Liked it too much.

On his way downstairs, he wondered whether he'd let her sleep for her. Or for himself. If he'd wakened her, he'd have wanted to kiss her. Again.

And again.

He didn't trust himself to take her mouth again. Not now, with the memory of her lips against his burned into his mind.

She awoke slowly, disoriented. The room wasn't familiar and, for a moment, she panicked, wondering where she was. When memory returned, with it came a smile.

Justin had asked her to read him a story.

Justin.

The sound of snoring nearby reassured her he was all right. Moonlight streaming in through the window highlighted his sweetly rounded cheeks and button nose. An angel in dinosaur pajamas. The image drew a smile from her.

"Good night, little angel," she whispered.

With a grimace for her sore neck, she rose and padded out of the room. An enticing aroma drew her downstairs to the kitchen.

A dish towel tied around his waist, Dave stood in front of the stove, stirring something.

"Smells good."

He turned, a smile of welcome on his face. She watched as the smile dimmed until it was only a shadow and a wariness appeared around his eyes. Before she had time to wonder at it, he gestured to the table. "If you don't mind leftovers, you're welcome to stay for supper."

"Sounds good. May I help?"

He hesitated before jerking his thumb toward the cupboards. "You can set the table if you'd like."

The words were cool, prompting her to make up an excuse that she needed to get home. Her stomach rumbled noisily, forestalling what she'd been about to say. The pizza dinner she'd shared with Justin was a long time ago. Dave had invited her for dinner. If he was regretting it now, that was his problem. Angling her chin, she found the dishes and set two places.

He ladled chunky stew into the bowls and placed a loaf of bread on the table. "Dig in."

She took a cautious bite. "It's good."

"You sound surprised."

"I am," she said frankly. "Most men don't cook like this." She took another bite and sighed appreciatively.

"That was me four years ago. Tuna fish sandwiches were the only things I didn't burn."

Four years ago — when his wife left. She nodded her understanding.

"You can do a lot of things when you have to," he said.

It didn't take much intuition to know he was talking about something far different than cooking. Something like getting along without a wife for him and a mother for Justin. Something like saying good-bye to her when the time came?

"Thank you for staying with Justin," he said.

The gratitude was genuine. She'd stake her life on it. But it was grudgingly given. He didn't want to be indebted to her. Not even in anything as simple as caring for his son while he was at work.

With a flash of insight, she realized that that was the last thing he'd want. Dave was willing to share himself, but his son was off-limits in their relationship.

She understood his need to protect Justin; what she didn't understand was why he felt he needed to protect him from her. Didn't he know she'd never hurt Justin?

A glance at the determined set of his jaw answered her question more clearly than words ever could. She decided to take a new tack.

"Your talk with Justin must have done the trick. He hasn't been in trouble in weeks. A lot of parents wouldn't take this much time to talk over their first-grader's problems. That's one of the reasons I admire you so much."

"Me?"

She nodded. "Your involvement with Justin, the way you are with your parents. Not everyone makes that kind of time or commitment to their family."

His eyes narrowed at that. How did she

know about his parents? Had she been pumping Justin about him? The lady knew entirely too much about him, and he wasn't comfortable with it.

"Justin told me how close you both are to them," she said. "I think that's pretty wonderful."

"You questioned my son?"

The warm interest in her eyes cooled. "I listen to him when he wants to talk. Is there something wrong with that?"

Too late he realized how accusing he must have sounded. "I didn't mean . . ." What had he meant?

"Look, if there's a problem with my talking with Justin about something other than school, I want to know."

"No problem," he said slowly. "I just don't want Justin to start depending on someone who isn't going to be around for the long haul."

"What're you talking about?"

"Nothing," he said shortly. "Nothing important."

"It's important enough to have you bite my head off for talking to Justin."

Is that what he'd done?

"Justin feels things deeply. He's already started to care about you. I just don't want to see him hurt."

"And you think I do?"

No. He didn't think that. He'd already seen how much she cared about his son. "I don't think you'd *mean* to hurt him."

"But you think I might end up hurting him anyway."

"I don't know." He shoved a hand through his hair, thinking that right now, he didn't know much of anything.

The exasperation in Katie's eyes confirmed she thought so too.

"I won't have him hurt," he said after long moments had passed. "You're here for a few months and then you'll be gone. And he'll be alone. Again."

"Maybe. Does that mean I can't care about him now? About you?"

"Justin's already had too many people leave him. He can't take someone else breezing in, saying she cares, and then taking off again."

"And you think that's what I'd do. That I'd hurt him?"

"I don't think you'd mean to," he repeated.

"Well, that makes me feel a lot better. I'm just too stupid to know what I'm doing. Is that it?"

"No." The word ripped from his throat. Why was she twisting everything around?

Couldn't she see that he just wanted to protect his son, to do what was best for him?

"Just because I look like your ex-wife doesn't mean I'd act like her."

The rational part of him knew that, but the past wielded a powerful hold.

She reached up to brush his cheek with the back of her hand. "You're a good man, Dave. And a good father. Maybe it's time you realized you can be both."

"What's that supposed to mean?"

"That you're afraid to let me too close. Afraid to care about me. Because if you do, you'll be vulnerable. And that's the one thing you can't bear. You've been the perfect single dad for so long that you're afraid to be anything else."

Her words cut too close to the truth, but he felt compelled to deny them anyway. "You're crazy, lady."

Abruptly, she pushed her bowl away and stood. "Am I? Ask yourself why you're afraid to let Justin be part of our relationship. Ask yourself why you won't let yourself enjoy what we have. When you come up with some answers, get back to me. I'm not going anywhere." She paused. "For now."

The significance of the last two words

wasn't lost on him. She'd all but said that she'd be patient, but not forever. Well, he couldn't blame her for that. He wasn't feeling very patient himself.

But he wasn't sure who his impatience was directed at — Katie or himself.

"Thanks for dinner."

"You're welcome."

He saw her to the door and helped her on with her coat, his hands lingering briefly on her shoulders. "Thanks again for staying with Justin."

"No problem." She couldn't keep the hurt from her voice. Right now, she didn't care.

"Katie . . ."

"Good-bye."

He stood there alone and wondered how he'd lost his cool so far as to jump all over Katie for something as innocent as talking to Justin. He had his reasons, but right now they seemed pretty flimsy. If he couldn't explain them to himself, how could he explain them to her? He'd felt alone when Marie left him, but the feeling didn't compare to what he felt now.

Outside, the wind whipped color into her cheeks, but she didn't feel the cold against her skin. Another kind of cold, one more stinging, more bitter, than the subzero temperature, had settled over her heart.

At home, she stripped off her coat and paced the apartment as hurt gave way to temper. For such a smart man, Dave had a lot to learn. How dare he imply she'd hurt his son, even unwittingly?

The furnace blasted heat into the apartment, but it couldn't ward off the cold that lodged in her heart. Even the memory of Justin trustingly curled up in her lap failed to warm her. She loved him as if he were her own. It was her bad luck that she also loved his father.

"Why won't you trust me?" The words were torn from her as tears dampened her cheeks.

Her only answer was the wail of the wind as it bawled its lament.

When morning came, she woke abruptly, chilled and stiff from sleeping on the sofa. She looked down to see that she still wore yesterday's clothes. A shower and fresh clothes freshened her appearance. If only they could cure what was wrong inside as well.

The children with their laughter, their uncomplicated joy in life, were the balm she needed. She threw herself into their play at recess with all the abandon of her most rambunctious first-grader.

When it was her turn at kickball, she booted the ball with the force of pent-up frustration. She ran the bases, her legs eating up the distance. The kids cheered as she reached home.

"Wow, Miss McGuire." Emilie shaded her eyes against the glare of the sun off the frost-covered ground. "You never kicked it that far before."

A smile nipped at Katie's mouth as she realized just what — or who — she'd wanted to kick. A certain engineer who couldn't see past the end of his nose. Temper simmered as she remembered his curt treatment of her last night. The words of gratitude had practically stuck in his throat.

When he appeared at her classroom at the end of the day, she wasn't surprised. Neither was she particularly pleased. If she'd entertained any hope that last night had changed how she felt about him, she'd been mistaken.

In a knit shirt and well-worn jeans, he looked incredible. But it wasn't his rugged good looks that had caused her to fall in love with him. Physical attraction was a lot easier to deal with than this deep, abiding need to be with him, to share life with him.

"Katie, we have to talk."

She looked up briefly before returning to grading her papers. "Do we?"

"I wanted to explain about last night."

"You made it clear you didn't want me being a part of Justin's life." She heard the stiffness in her voice and hated it but was powerless to prevent it.

He took her hand. "Please. Hear me out. That's all I'm asking."

Reason warned her to refuse, but her heart rejected that judgment. She put down the red pencil she was using to mark papers and sat back in her chair. Waiting.

"You have to understand what it was like when Marie left. She wasn't much of a wife, even less of a mother, but she was something. Justin cried for her for weeks . . . months . . . after she left. I promised myself I'd never let anyone hurt him like that again."

Her heart ached at the pain in his voice, but she wouldn't take the blame for something his ex-wife had done.

"I'm not Marie," she said with quiet emphasis.

He stared at her for long minutes before slowly nodding. "No, you're not."

"Then stop judging me by her."

"Is that what I've been doing?"

She didn't answer but let him figure it out by himself.

"You should've told me to get lost," he said, a wry smile touching his lips.

"I thought about it a couple of times," she admitted, feeling the beginnings of a smile of her own.

"Only a couple?"

The dimple winked as her smile blossomed. "Well, maybe a few more than that."

"How many more?" he teased.

"Don't push your luck."

The tension between them dissolved with that, and he pulled her into his arms.

"Can we start over? Say tonight?" he asked, his warm breath a soft caress against her cheek.

"I'd like that." She lifted her lips, a silent invitation.

He lowered his head and brushed a kiss across her mouth. It was a whisper, a just-barely-there kiss that shook her all the way down to her toes. It shouldn't have, that chaste meeting of lips.

It shouldn't have, but it did.

That evening, she listened as Dave tried to untangle his feelings. The words came haltingly, as though he were trying to understand them himself even as he explained them to her.

"Marie was beautiful. The most beautiful woman I'd ever seen. I was bewitched the moment I saw her." He took Katie's hand in his, tracing the fine networking of veins visible beneath the fair skin.

"I thought I was the luckiest man in the world when she said yes when I asked her out. We started seeing each other every chance we could. The business had just taken off. I was so full of myself that I believed her when she said she loved me."

"Maybe she did."

He fitted a finger beneath her chin, lifting it so that their eyes met. "You say that because you can't imagine saying those words without meaning them. Marie's not like that. She knew exactly what she wanted. Someone on the way up."

"No." She was barely aware of saying the word. No one could be that calculating, that cold.

"Yes. She told me after we got married. She might have stayed around longer if she hadn't become pregnant right away. She didn't like being sick and hated losing her figure. She blamed me for both." Bitterness carved harsh lines around his eyes. "I was naïve enough to hope she'd change once she saw the baby . . . our baby.

"She wasn't much of a mother. She'd take off whenever the mood hit her. One night I came home and found Justin alone." He shoved a hand through his hair. "He wasn't much more than a baby and she left him by himself."

Her gasp went unnoticed as he continued. "I hired a nanny to stay with him. Within a year, Marie was gone. She couldn't get away fast enough when she made up her mind. She stuck around just long enough to make sure she got a settlement big enough to tide her over until she found her next meal ticket.

"Justin wasn't much over two years old, but he kept asking for her, asking when Mommy was coming back."

Her heart wept silently at the picture he painted.

"After she left, I didn't know what to do. Literally. I just about went crazy trying to take care of Justin and keep up the house and still manage the business."

She heard the bitterness, and more, the self-blame. His sense of responsibility was such that he would always shoulder the blame. She suspected he could forgive Marie much more easily than he ever could himself that their marriage didn't work out.

"I let Justin down." His voice broke and so did her heart.

"You did everything you could."

"No." The laugh that escaped was harsh and bleak. "I didn't. I wasn't there for Justin when he needed me most. I'm still not there."

"You're there for him in all the important ways, all the ways that count." She took his hand and rubbed it against her cheek. "Marie didn't deserve you. Or Justin. Leaving you and Justin . . . that's her loss."

The grimness around his eyes eased. "You're right — about Justin anyway. He's the best part of me, the only thing Marie and I ever did right together."

The sincerity in his voice caused her heart to melt a little more. His love for his son was there in everything he said, everything he did. For a moment, she was envious, wondering what it would have been like to know that kind of love as a child.

Her own father had been kind enough in an absentminded way. A science professor at a small college, he hadn't quite known what to do with a child after her mother had died. When he remembered, he asked her how her day was. Sometimes, he even waited while she told him. But she'd known his mind was elsewhere, with his students and the next journal paper he planned to publish.

She'd soon learned to keep anything important to herself. It was easier . . . and less painful . . . than hoping he'd listen, really listen, to the hurts and fears, joys and hopes, of a small girl. They'd gotten along well enough after that. As long as she didn't expect anything beyond mild interest, she'd been able to keep her disappointment to a minimum.

They still kept in touch. Christmas cards, calls on birthdays, the occasional letter. But the contact was that of two people bound by habit rather than love.

Love, real love, wasn't a habit, but a joy. It was that joy, that gut-deep joy, she saw in Dave's eyes whenever he talked about his son. She knew him well enough to know he'd give that same love to a woman. If he let himself.

"Katie?"

She looked up.

"Where'd you go?" Amusement tinged with concern colored his voice.

A flush, the curse of fair skin, heated her cheeks. "Sorry. I was thinking."

"Want to share?" He sounded like he really wanted to know.

"I was just thinking how lucky Justin is to have a dad like you. Someone who's there for him."

She watched with interest as color crept up his neck and face. When was the last time she'd seen a man blush? It was endearing. It made him appear vulnerable, more human.

"Even when I've been a total jerk to you, you really mean that, don't you?"

"Yeah," she said with a smile. "I do."

"You're a classy lady, Katie McGuire."

Her color deepened as he skimmed his knuckles down her jaw. He followed the trail with his lips. This time the kiss wasn't casual. It didn't whisper; it shouted.

The analogy wasn't lost on her as her feelings reached a crescendo pitch. When he lifted his head, she felt a sigh shudder from her.

"I care about you, Katie," he said, the hoarseness of his voice telling her more than words.

She did a lot more than care about him. She was in love. With him and Justin both. She consoled herself with the reminder that caring was the first step to love.

Their relationship took a new turn after that. Maybe, she thought, he had finally accepted that she wasn't his ex-wife. Whatever the reasons, she could only be grateful that he had relaxed around her enough to let Justin become part of their relationship.

When a teachers' seminar took Katie out of town over the weekend, Dave insisted upon driving her. When he arrived to pick her up, Justin was in the backseat.

"Isn't this great, Mith McGuire? We get to drive all the way to St. Louis together. Then Dad and I are gonna spend the night in a motel and take you back in the morning."

She turned questioning eyes on Dave. "You don't have to stay. I can take the bus back."

"We want to," Dave said, stowing her overnight case in the back of the truck.

"Yeah," Justin added. "We want to."

She kissed his cheek.

"Hey, don't I get one of those?" Dave asked.

Her lips curved into a smile as she brushed them across his cheek.

"That's not quite what I had in mind," he said in a low voice.

"Later," she promised, her smile broadening.

She had to spend the day in classes. When she arrived back at the college dorm where the teachers attending the seminar were staying, she found Dave and Justin waiting for her.

"Dad's taking us out for dinner," Justin said. "He's letting me choose."

Dave rolled his eyes. "I plead temporary insanity."

A frown settled on Justin's lips. "What's temp . . . temp . . . what's that thing?"

"It means he loves you a lot," Katie said, sending Dave a reproving look.

The frown vanished, to be replaced by a face-splitting grin. "I know that. Dad tells me every day."

Justin chose a pizza parlor with video arcades and a playland that resembled a giant gerbil trail. Tinny music and children's laughter filled the air. Dave ordered an extra-large pizza-with-the-works and a pitcher of root beer.

Justin spent a minimum of time shoving pizza into his mouth and washing it down with root beer before pushing away his plate. "Can I have some quarters, Dad?"

Katie fought a grin as she watched Dave dig into his pockets and produce a handful of change. Justin had his dad well trained.

Face covered with gooey cheese and tomato sauce, Justin scampered off.

Dave exchanged a wry smile with Katie. "This isn't exactly my idea of a romantic evening."

"It's a family evening."

The smile wiped from his face for an instant before reappearing. "Yeah. A family evening."

She couldn't forget his reaction that night after he dropped her off at the dorm. She wondered if Dave would ever be able to accept her fully. She knew he still had reservations about letting her into his life. She'd hoped . . . prayed . . . that she was gradually defeating his fears.

Time and patience could overcome almost anything, she reminded herself. Fortunately, she had plenty of both.

Chapter Six

A few days before Thanksgiving vacation, Mrs. Carrot Top delivered six babies. The children were thrilled, the father looked proud, and Katie wondered how she'd ended up nursemaid to six baby rabbits. A consultation with a pet shop owner netted her the information that the babies could be removed from their mother and each other after five weeks.

"Gross," Tyler said, watching as Mrs. Carrot Top scratched off pieces of fur.

"Double gross," Justin echoed.

"That's how she builds her nest," Katie explained.

The rabbits were the main topic of conversation over the next few days. Katie dragged the two cages home with her for the holiday. Next year, she promised herself, she'd look into a tropical fish as the class pet.

The Saturday following Thanksgiving, Katie and Dave planned to spend the afternoon Christmas shopping. The delicatessen Dave took her to for lunch smelled of salami and ham, German potato salad and dill pickles. She sniffed appreciatively and ordered a salami on rye with extra mustard. Dave got the same with a side order of potato salad.

They lingered over the meal.

"What's Justin want for Christmas this year?" she asked.

"That's just it. I don't know."

"Most kids have made a dozen lists by now."

"Last year he handed me a list a foot long." A smile brushed his lips as he remembered the misspelled words. "This year he said he didn't want anything."

"Nothing?"

"He said Santa knew what he wanted and I didn't have to worry about it." He rubbed his jaw. "I don't get it."

"Be thankful," she said. "Most of the kids in my class are so hyped up by TV commercials that they want every toy ever created."

"That bad, huh?"

She grimaced. "That bad. So what are you getting him?"

"A new bike. He's outgrown the one he has. Maybe some new computer games."

Her lips twitched with the need to grin. "No underwear and socks?"

He made a face. "You sound like my

mom. She's always buying those for me."

A laugh bubbled out despite her best efforts to contain it. She clapped a hand to her mouth.

"You think that's funny, huh?"

"No, I think it's sweet."

"I guess buying underwear and socks is what moms are for."

"And the dads get to buy all the fun things like bikes and computer games."

He grinned. "That's what dads are for."

With a startled rush, she realized how intimate the conversation had become. Intimate in the sense that she wanted to be part of that buying ritual. Intimate in the sense that she wanted to be part of a family. Intimate in the sense that she wanted Dave and Justin to be that family.

"We better get started," she said, pushing her plate away and scooting out from the booth.

Dave gave her a quizzical look but didn't say anything at her abrupt end to the conversation.

Dave found a miniature mountain bike and helmet which he stowed in the car. She found a scholarly book for her father and a dinosaur video game for Justin. After agonizing over it, she chose a hand-knit sweater for Dave.

Four hours later, she dropped gratefully onto a bench in the inside courtyard of the mall. "And I thought teaching was hard work. It's a snap compared to this." She gestured to the body-to-body crowd of holiday shoppers.

"You're not wimping out already, are you?"

She pantomimed a heart attack and collapsed against him.

"Okay, okay. I get the message. What would it take to revive you?"

"A Mrs. Fields cookie," she said immediately. "White chocolate chip with macadamia nuts."

"Don't tell me; let me guess. It's a new cure for mall burnout." He kissed the tip of her nose. "Be right back."

She eased off one boot and then the other. By the time Dave was back, she was wiggling her argyle-clad toes.

"Your cookie fix," he said, presenting a white bakery bag, warm and fragrant, to her.

She peeked inside to find a dozen cookies. "I've died and gone to heaven." She bit into a cookie with all the pleasure of a child given a special treat.

Dave watched, his smile indulgent and tender. Spending time with Katie had soon become a habit. A very enjoyable habit. He hadn't intended to like her company so much. But it was hard to resist a woman who took such pleasure in the simple activities they'd shared.

The shopping trip had been her idea when she heard he was worried about what to get Justin for Christmas. It was like her to want to help him.

With her help, he'd found the perfect bike. In addition, they'd bought the food processor his mom had been hinting for and a new fly-fishing rod for his dad. When he asked about shopping for her family, she said there was just her dad.

He wondered about that. For someone who so obviously enjoyed family life, Katie never mentioned her father. Was there some kind of estrangement there, or had they gradually drifted apart? The idea of not having his parents in his and Justin's lives was unthinkable.

Back at her apartment, she heated cider, adding cinnamon sticks to it. The fragrant aroma filled the kitchen. It was the kind of homey touch he'd come to expect from Katie.

They carried mugs of hot cider into the living room.

"I don't ever want to move again," she

said, settling onto the sofa and toeing her boots off. "Can we just stay this way forever?"

It was tempting, he thought, leaning over to brush a kiss against her hair. It smelled of the winter air and some kind of fruity shampoo. The combination was heady.

She returned the kiss, her lips soft and giving beneath his.

At home, he let himself remember the feel of Katie nestled in his arms, the touch of her lips against his. She was in his mind, his heart, his very soul. He doubted he'd ever be free of her.

Would that be so bad?

The question came out of nowhere, startling him. When had he started thinking in terms of a future with Katie? When had the word forever become part of his thinking? Because that's what he wanted with her.

"You've got it bad, man," he said in the emptiness of the night. "Real bad."

She scared him right down to his toes.

He got a hold of himself. He had no reason to be afraid. She was a little slip of a woman, after all. She couldn't do anything he didn't let her.

The exclamation of disgust startled him before he realized it had come from him.

Who was he trying to fool? She'd already done it. She'd made herself a place in his heart with no more effort than a child gave love.

He'd warned himself against caring, against falling for her, but his heart had refused to listen. Could it work? The question had been there all the time, he realized, teasing his imagination and causing his heart to beat a rapid tattoo against his chest.

"I need you," he whispered, his voice little more than a rasp of sound. "I need you, Katie."

Three Saturdays before Christmas, Katie, Justin, and Dave headed to the mountains to find a Christmas tree. With snowshoes strapped to their boots, they tramped through knee-high drifts in search of the perfect tree.

Katie pointed out several trees, each one of them rejected by either Dave or Justin as too small, too skinny, too *something*. Accustomed to buying a tree from the supermarket lot, she wasn't prepared for the critical scrutiny they bestowed upon each possibility.

Finally Justin pointed to a towering fir. "This one."

Dave and Katie exchanged grins. It was the biggest tree they'd encountered — undoubtedly the reason Justin had chosen it.

"Okay," Dave said. "Let's get to work." He nicked the spot he wanted to make the cut and then ordered them to stand clear.

He stripped off his coat. Even through his flannel shirt, the bunching and releasing of hard-toned muscles was evident. Katie kept her attention on Justin, but she couldn't help a few stray glances in Dave's direction. He swung the ax with a rhythmic motion that had its own kind of grace.

Halfway through the task, he shed his flannel shirt, leaving on only a T-shirt. She shivered in her down coat as sweat glistened on his forehead and arms.

"Keep back," he yelled.

After assuring himself that Katie and Justin had retreated well away, he gave a final chop. The tree quivered for a moment in the still morning air before tumbling to the earth. The ground trembled beneath the crash. Instinctively, Katie drew Justin closer to her.

The tree looked even bigger now that it was sprawled on the ground, and Katie shuddered at the thought of trying to drag it back to the truck. Some of her worry must have shown in her eyes, for Dave grinned.

"Don't ever go into undercover work," he said.

The abrupt statement had her head jerking up. "Why?"

"Your eyes give you away every time."

"Okay, Mr. Mind Reader, what was I thinking?"

"You're wondering how we're going to get this back to the truck. Right?"

"Right," came her grudging response.

"Watch."

To Justin's complaints, Dave took off three feet of trunk and stripped off some of the bottom branches. The tree looked a lot more manageable after that. He pulled back on his shirt and coat before announcing it was time to eat.

After snacking on doughnuts and hot chocolate from a thermos she'd brought along, they played snow tag. Katie grinned as Dave whooped and hollered as loudly as Justin.

"Gotcha," she said, laughing at the surprise on Dave's face as she caught him with a snowball.

"You're asking for it," he warned.

She lobbed another one, her aim perfect as it hit him squarely in the chest.

The look in his eyes promised retribution. "You've done it now." He rolled a snowball between his gloved hands and took aim.

She took refuge behind a tree.

Justin squealed as Dave purposefully headed in her direction.

Laughing too hard to run, she collapsed against the tree, shielding her face with her hands.

"You're dead meat, McGuire," he said, advancing on her.

Justin danced around, his eyes bright with excitement, cheeks red with cold. "Dad, take it easy on her. She's a *girl*." The last word came out in a hushed tone that had both Katie and Dave grinning.

"I don't know," he said, looming over Katie, the snowball still in hand.

"Please," she begged, pretending to cower in fear even as she picked up some snow.

He pulled her up hard against his chest and kissed her. She clung to him, uncaring of the cold, uncaring of anything but the man who held her as if he'd never let her go. Ragged breaths came in icy plumes.

"Hey, what're you guys doing?" Justin yelled, clearly put out at the interruption of the game.

His shout shattered the mood. With her arms wound around Dave's neck, she shoved the snow down his parka.

He bellowed as the snow worked its way down his back. "That's war, lady."

The snowball fight began in earnest, with Justin and Katie teaming up against Dave. They were fairly evenly matched. She gave as good as she got until she noticed Justin shivering. Her eyes signaled the message to Dave.

"I think we'd better call it a day," he said.

"Aw, Dad."

"Katie's getting cold."

Justin cast a disparaging look at Katie even as his teeth chattered. "Okay."

"Thanks for making me the wimp of the piece," she whispered to Dave.

"Hey, we're big, macho guys. We can't admit to being cold." He drew her to him. "Maybe you can warm me up," he said, wriggling his eyebrows suggestively.

She punched him in the arm, which he immediately clutched and yowled in pain.

When Justin wrapped his arms around their legs, they toppled to the ground. She lay there against Dave's chest, feeling the rapid beat of his heart beneath his heavy coat.

"Truce?" he asked.

"Truce." She pushed up to brace herself

on her elbows. Her gaze caught and held Dave's. What she saw in his eyes caused her breath to stop in her throat. He cared about her. He couldn't look at her like that if he didn't care.

Justin squirmed in the tangle of bodies. "I'm getting squished."

Katie rolled away and stood. A glance at Dave confirmed he shared her reluctance to end the contact.

They dragged the tree back to the truck, exhausted but happy.

"Can we do this again?" Justin asked on the way home.

"Cut down a Christmas tree?" Dave teased.

"Dad." The word held a wealth of six-year-old exasperation. "We can't cut down another tree. We already got one."

"What do you want to do again?" Katie asked gently.

"Be together," the little boy said simply. "The three of us. Like we are now."

"I'd like that too," she said with a glance toward Dave.

His hands had tightened on the steering wheel, but he said nothing.

A bit of the brightness slipped from the day just as the sun slipped behind the clouds.

The secret hope she'd harbored for the last few weeks poked its head out, forcing her to admit that she wanted more than a few outings with Dave and Justin. She wanted a happily-ever-after ending like the ones in the fairy tales she read to her first-graders. She wanted a lifetime of todays.

Dave answered a seemingly never-ending string of questions from Justin, but his mind was on Katie. She was quiet for the trip back to town. When Justin dozed, his head snuggled against her shoulder, an awkward silence settled over them. It stretched tautly between them until the tension became unbearable. Dave chanced a glance at her, only to be greeted by a remote profile. Gone was the happy, laughing woman of only an hour ago.

He knew she was hurt over his lack of response to Justin's simple suggestion that they do this again. The truth was, he wanted it more than he cared to admit.

Justin made no secret over his feelings for Katie. Dave had given up trying to keep them apart. Could he too be falling in love with the pretty teacher?

It wasn't hard to picture himself in love with her. She was beautiful and smart, compassionate and strong. She was also opinionated, stubborn, and independent to a fault. He was fascinated and charmed, exasperated and disturbed in turns. But never bored.

Marie had bored him within weeks of their marriage. Her excessive interest in her looks, her insistence that they go out every evening, had quickly worn thin. He couldn't imagine Katie preoccupied with such superficial matters.

Still, the rational part of his mind, the part that designed software and demanded logical answers to questions, insisted he couldn't be in love with her. He'd known her less than two months. Heck, he hadn't even kissed her properly yet.

With Marie, he'd been certain that he loved her within hours of meeting her. He'd thought he was immune to those feelings now, the heady sense of wanting and needing and loving. He'd promised himself that he wouldn't make that mistake again. Now, here he was, more cautious certainly, more wary, but in love just the same.

"I . . . uh . . . I'm glad you could come today," he said, hearing the inadequacy of his words but unable to come up with anything better.

She nodded briefly.

When they reached her building, she let herself out quickly. "Don't bother coming in. You don't want to wake up Justin."

Now it was his turn to nod. And feel even more miserable than she looked.

When Dave turned up that night, she was prepared. She'd done a lot of thinking during the afternoon and realized she couldn't handle the level of hot-and-cold-running feelings Dave seemed determined to keep their relationship at.

"I wanted to explain . . . about today . . ." He looked so miserable that she was tempted to let him off the hook.

Then again, it was a time for openness. Coming to terms with his feelings was as necessary for Dave as it was for her. And so she waited.

"I like being with you, Katie. I like it a lot." He looked at her as though willing her to say something.

Still, she remained silent.

"I like having you around."

She barely refrained from socking him in the arm. He made her sound like a faithful dog or maybe a comfortable old chair. That was hardly the feeling she'd been hoping for.

Apparently he realized how it must have sounded, for he groaned and shoved his fingers through his hair. "That didn't come out the way I meant."

"What *did* you mean, Dave?" she asked quietly.

He paused. "I like how you make me feel, how I feel when I'm with you."

"What about Justin?"

This time the pause lengthened. The silence stretched taut. Just when she decided he wasn't going to give her an answer, he said, "I know you care about Justin and that he feels the same about you."

"And you don't like that?"

"It's not that. It's just . . ."

"You don't want him hurt."

"Yeah."

The word was filled with such pain and fear that she didn't have the heart to remind him that she'd never hurt his son. Maybe someday he'd realize that all by himself.

She said the only thing that mattered. "I love you."

The look on his face would have been comical if she'd been in a mood to be amused. Instead, she could only regret that he couldn't accept what she gave.

A more sophisticated woman might have kept her feelings to herself, but Katie had never seen any reason to hide what she felt. She wasn't any good at it, so she didn't even try. She'd always believed feelings were meant to be shared. If Dave couldn't handle hers, she could accept that.

What she couldn't accept was burying those feelings. That would be dishonest, and the one thing she wouldn't do was lie to Dave. Or to herself.

Dishonesty never solved anything. She'd learned that lesson a year ago when she'd tried to make herself over into what her fiancé had wanted. She'd ended up despising him, and, even worse, hating herself.

Dave went very still. His face, his hands, even his body, appeared to have become frozen. He said nothing.

"Is something wrong?" She grazed her knuckle down his cheek, the caress as natural as breathing. "There's nothing to look so scared about."

Was that what he was feeling? Scared? Scared didn't begin to cover it.

He couldn't continue simply to stare at her. He had to say something, even if the words weren't those he knew she wanted to hear. "Look, Katie, you're a very emotional person. What you're feeling now is . . ."

"Love," she supplied, her smile easy. "Taking love's easy. Giving it is a bit harder, but you don't have to worry about that." She spread her hands wide. "Please, take it for what it is. A gift."

Her eyes were wide with honesty. He didn't doubt she believed what she said. What he did doubt was how long that love would last. Love, the forever kind like his parents had, was so rare as to be an endangered species.

If it were just himself, he might take a chance on it. But he had Justin to think about. Justin didn't need any more upsets in his life. He'd already had one mother desert him; Dave wasn't about to take a chance on repeating that.

Her smile wobbled around the edges but was still intact. "You don't want even that, do you?"

"I . . ." He fumbled for words and found none, at least none that were adequate.

"Love doesn't need to be returned to exist."

There it was again. That honesty of hers. She didn't play games. It was but one more reminder that she was nothing like Marie. But it didn't change things between them. He *couldn't* let it change things.

"I won't apologize for my feelings," she said. "I'm not ashamed of them."

She wouldn't be. It was one of the things he loved most about her. The easy use of the word startled him. Before he could consider the implications, she was kissing him lightly.

"The gift'll still be there. Whenever you're ready to take it."

She made it sound so easy. Like all he had to do was rip the paper off a box and there was this wonderful present inside. The trouble was, the kind of gift Katie was offering came with its own set of complications, complications he wasn't sure he was ready to deal with.

He looked at the love shining from her eyes. Maybe it was as easy as she made it seem. Maybe. . . .

On the way home, he mentally kicked himself for not handling the situation with more finesse. Katie gave love because that was her way. He'd all but thrown it back at her. Even if he didn't believe in it for himself, that was no reason to belittle what she felt.

Katie had said that she loved him. Once before he'd believed a woman who whispered those words to him.

Had he loved Marie? He'd thought so. He'd given his heart with the eagerness that only the young — or the very naïve — brought to love. He'd been both.

Now he was neither young nor naïve. Marie had destroyed those qualities with the same ruthlessness with which she'd wiped out his bank account.

He didn't understand love, at least not in the way Katie defined it. No, he didn't understand it, and he wanted no part of it. All he wanted was peace.

Peace? his mind questioned. Or security? Weren't they one and the same? And neither had anything to do with love. He wondered why he was having such a hard time convincing himself of it.

Katie didn't let Dave's reaction to her declaration get her down. He'd been hurt in the past and didn't want to love her, even though she was pretty sure he already did. But, even if she misread him completely, she didn't regret loving him. Her love was a gift, freely given. If he couldn't accept it, better she know that now.

She threw herself into preparations for the Christmas program. Given a choice, she'd take action over brooding any day.

She was knee-deep in pasting paper tree ornaments on a huge cardboard tree when she got the call over the intercom system to come to the office. After making sure her teaching aide could manage, she hurried to the office.

"You wanted to see me, Mrs. Michaels?" she asked the principal.

She liked the principal, a tiny woman who inspired enthusiasm in others with her positive attitude.

"It's about one of the children in your class. Justin Chase." She looked at her notes. "He appears to be having a rough year. I wanted to hear your thoughts on the subject."

Briefly, Katie outlined Justin's misbehavior. "I talked with Dave . . . Mr. Chase, Justin's father. Justin's been a lot better since then."

"That's fine. He's a sweet child. I'm glad you're on top of things."

Katie thought about that on her way back to her classroom. Was she on top of things, as the principal had said? She'd never understood what had prompted Justin's behavior. Something had triggered it. A child didn't act up for no reason.

The strains of "Jingle Bell Rock" drifted from the classroom, and she felt her spirits lift. No one could remain depressed while listening to the pure, sweet voices of children.

"You all sound great," she said, smiling at the teaching aide. "Now let's go down to the gym. We need to practice on the stage."

Accompanied by a lot of giggling and

whispering, they trooped down to the combination gymnasium-cafeteria that sported a makeshift stage.

"Candy canes over here," Katie said, pointing to her right. "Gumdrops on the other side. Angels, behind the candy canes."

Thirty-two shy, excited first-graders shuffled their way across the stage, their movements hampered only slightly by their costumes. The Christmas program was only two days away. Right now, two months wouldn't be enough time to prepare.

A fleeting smile chased away Katie's worries. The program always managed to come together at the last minute. This year would be no exception . . . she hoped.

When they finished with "Silent Night," tears pricked her eyes.

"Wonderful," she said after the closing note. "Your parents are going to be so proud of you."

She worked late that night, making last-minute adjustments to angel wings and candy cane costumes. When Dave didn't call, she wasn't surprised.

She'd scared him. She only hoped he'd trust his feelings enough to accept the love she'd offered. Trust wasn't something he gave easily. Even to himself.

Chapter Seven

She was in his thoughts far too much. Sometimes, when she slipped into his mind, she was sitting with a child on her lap, reading quietly. At other times, she was playing outside, kicking a ball, as caught up in the game as any of her first-graders. At still others, she was laughing, her eyes sparkling at him, her soft lips turned up in a smile that never failed to turn him inside out.

He hadn't taken the meat out to thaw for dinner. A mountain of laundry towered by the washer in the utility room. And Justin's program was tonight.

Nearly incoherent with excitement, Justin bullied Dave into changing and leaving for the school before he could fix anything for dinner. Dave consoled himself with the thought that they'd pick up something on the way. Munching on a cardboard hamburger that they'd ordered in the drive-through of a fast-food place, he wondered when life had gotten so complicated.

Still, he couldn't regret that tonight was the Christmas program. It meant another chance to see Katie. They'd arranged to go out for dessert following the program.

"Come on, Dad," Justin urged after they'd parked the car. "Mith McGuire says we're s'pposed to be there early."

When his shepherd's robe caught in the car door, Justin was close to tears. They managed to avert catastrophe when Dave extracted the terry-cloth robe, a refugee from his closet, without tearing it. They found the room the first-graders were to meet in. After giving Justin a final kiss and hug, Dave headed out to the auditorium.

The stage had been transformed into a Christmas wonderland. Combined with the holiday music and the sweet voices of children, it took him back to his own childhood, where all things were possible.

For the first time he let himself picture a future with Katie. They'd be a family, the kind he'd always dreamed of. There'd be more children, a house full of children.

He wanted, years from now, to be able to look back and recall shared memories, the joys and sorrows of a lifetime spent together. It wasn't the head-over-heels feeling he'd experienced for Marie. It was a deep, abiding need to grow with her, to have children with her, to build a life with her.

He knew she loved him and Justin. He

loved them both. There. He'd finally admitted it. All that remained was to ask her to marry him.

The program passed in a blur for him, his mind on Katie. After dropping Justin off at his parents' house, he drove to her apartment. He knocked on the door and heard her call, "Come in."

"Be right out," she said.

He smiled, remembering the first time he'd come to pick her up for a date. He'd found the door open then just as it was tonight.

He hadn't meant to snoop. He'd picked up a paperback thriller left on a side table and started to flip through it when a letter fell out. Folded in thirds, its bottom third opened to reveal words Dave couldn't help but see.

"Hope to see you back in Chicago in January."

He angrily shoved the letter back in the book without reading more. Katie had never said anything about leaving at the end of the term. She'd never said anything about leaving, period. In fairness, he'd never asked. But one would think she'd have mentioned something about it.

But no, she hadn't said a word.

What else had she lied about?

The question came out of left field, but he couldn't dismiss it.

When Katie reappeared, more lovely than ever in pink wool pants and matching sweater, he slapped the book down with guilty haste.

"Sorry to keep you waiting," she said, slipping her arms around him.

"No problem," he said, gently disengaging himself. "Look, I just remembered something I've got to take care of."

"That's all right. I'll wait. Or maybe I could go with you."

"It's probably going to take all night. I'll call you, okay?" He kissed her cheek, knowing he was taking the coward's way out, but he had to get away from her before he did something stupid, like begging her to stay.

"Sure." The puzzled look in her eyes caused him to hesitate.

He knew she was confused. So was he. But he couldn't spend the rest of the evening with her. Not until he got some things figured out. Not until he understood what was happening.

The letter said it all. Katie was leaving in January. She'd said all the right things, told him and Justin that she loved them, and then was going to leave without so much as telling him.

He spent the next three days making excuses to avoid seeing her. When she showed up that night, bearing a gift, he knew the time had come to have it out.

"Dad, it's Mith McGuire," Justin called from the door.

Not ready for what he had to do, Dave could only stare at her. Flecks of snow glimmered against her hair, a million diamonds caught in strands of spun gold. Her cheeks pink from the cold, she shook the snow from her boots.

"May I come in?" she asked when he still hadn't found his voice.

"Uh, sure." He stepped back to make room for her.

"I just stopped by to give Justin this." She handed Justin a gaily wrapped present.

"Wow! Can I open it now?"

"Sure."

He tore the ribbon and ripped the paper, his hands quick and sure as he pulled out a book on dinosaurs. "Thanks, Mith McGuire. You remembered."

"Of course I remembered. How could I forget that you love dinosaurs?"

"Are you getting me something else too?" he asked.

She smiled mysteriously. "Could be."

Justin threw his arms around her legs.

Caught off balance, she felt herself falling. A muscular arm snaked around her waist, bringing her up against a hard chest.

"Thanks." Her smile, the one that worked its way from her lips to her eyes, sparkled up at him.

Dave held her close, unable to bring himself to release her. She felt so good, so *right*, there in his arms. He ached to kiss those sweetly curved lips, ached to tell her what he knew she wanted to hear. He could do neither, so he did what he had to.

He let her go.

It was the hardest thing he'd ever had to do. His breath came in short, hard pants as if he'd sprinted through the night's subzero temperature.

He had to tell her. But first he had to get Justin out of the room. He hunted for an excuse and grabbed at the first one that came to mind.

"Hey, partner, why don't you change into your pajamas and then get us some of those cookies your grandma gave us?"

Justin scooted out of the room.

"I love this time of year," Katie said, twirling around the room, her arms spread wide. "The smells, the sights, the sounds — everything."

The Christmas lights danced over her

hair, her face, a kaleidoscope of ever-changing colors. They paled, though, against the happiness that shimmered in her eyes. He forced his attention back to what needed to be done.

He caught her hands in his, bringing her to a halt. "We need to talk."

Her lips slightly parted, she looked up at him, her eyes wide and questioning.

"You and me . . . I think we've been moving too fast."

"Too fast?"

"We're getting ahead of ourselves."

"Why don't you say what you mean," she said evenly.

"All right." He shoved a hand through his hair. "How long do you plan on staying here?"

The question plainly surprised her, for her eyes widened. "How long?"

"Yeah. Are you going to teach for the rest of the school year? Two years? Or are you heading back to Chicago when the term's over?" He willed her to deny it.

"I don't know."

"But you're thinking about it."

"I've got a lot of ties there."

"What about your ties here?" He could have kicked himself for asking that, but he couldn't help it. He needed to know. For

Justin's sake. For his own.

"What about them? Are you asking if I have ties here? If so, the answer's yes. I love my kids here. I love Justin. I — " Whatever she'd been about to say, she thought better about it.

"You what?"

"Nothing."

"I don't think we should see each other anymore."

Katie dropped the piece of wrapping paper she held in her hand. "You don't want to see me anymore?" The words came slowly, as if she were testing them for some hidden meaning.

"We'll see each other at school things. Like last night."

"But not outside school? Is that right?"

His silence was answer enough.

"Why, Dave?" she asked. "Why do you want to send me away?"

If he'd been a braver man, if life had dealt him a different hand, he'd have reached for her and taken her in his arms. He'd have kissed away the pain he saw in her face. But he'd learned not to believe what he read in a woman's eyes, what he heard in her voice. He'd learned the hard way.

"I think it's best," he said at last.

"Best for you? Me? Or Justin? That's it,

isn't it? You don't want me getting too close to your son."

"I have to think of him," he said, more harshly than he intended. "I'm afraid we're sending him mixed signals. I don't want him getting the wrong idea."

"What wrong idea would that be?" she asked in a dangerously quiet voice.

"That you and I . . . that we . . ."

"That we care about each other, that we love each other," she finished for him.

"I never said anything about love." And he hadn't, he told himself, ignoring the prick of self-righteousness. He'd been very careful to keep the L-word out of his relationship with Katie. But he hadn't been able to keep it out of his thoughts.

"No, *I* did. Is that what this is really about? You couldn't handle it when I told you that I loved you."

"That's got nothing to do with it. This is about Justin. I won't have him hurt. Not again."

He stared at her, seeing the trembling of her lips, the glistening moisture in her eyes, and somewhere deep inside, the hurt. Hurt he'd put there.

He hardened his heart against it. He wasn't the one who was leaving. She was. With that fixed in his mind, he was able to make himself say what he needed to.

"You said yourself you don't know how long you'll be here."

"Don't you see? What I do depends on . . ."

"What?"

"What happens between us."

He had some idea what the admission cost her. He knew because he didn't have the guts to make a similar one. Besides, he had Justin to think about. Whatever was between himself and Katie, Justin had to come first.

He wanted to touch her. Wanted it so bad he could taste it. But he kept his distance. If he touched her, he'd never be able to keep his mind on what mattered most.

"You kissed me like you . . ." Her unspoken words hung in the air between them, a silent accusation.

He couldn't bear to hear his foolishness recounted. "I know what I said. What I did. I was wrong." There. He'd said it. She couldn't fault him for his honesty. "I can't let you . . . anyone . . . disrupt our lives."

"Is that what I am? A disruption?"

He held out his hands, the gesture one of appeal and resignation. "I never meant it to go this far."

"You never meant. What does that mean? That you allowed yourself to care for me only so much and no more? That you can turn your feelings on and off like a faucet? Well, I can't." Her chin went up. "I won't apologize for it."

She wouldn't. He respected her for that. That didn't mean he could let her into their lives. Correction — he already had. But he intended to change that. For Justin's sake, he had to.

For Justin's, or for his own? a small voice asked. He ignored that. She didn't understand how deep his desire ran to protect his son, how much he was willing to do to safeguard Justin from pain.

"I won't be stopping by again," she said. "You don't need to worry. I can't keep from seeing Justin in class, but I'll keep my distance."

He couldn't deny the pain he heard in her voice. It was too real to be faked. "I don't want — "

"You don't want. You don't care. You don't need." She punctuated each word with a jab to his chest. "Well, let me tell you something, Mr. Dave Chase. Right now, I don't give diddly-squat what you want or don't want. You got that?"

Fury supplanted the hurt in her eyes.

"Katie, don't go like this."

"You lost the chance to ask me anything," she said, and shot past him.

"Mith McGuire, where're you going?" Justin asked, carrying a tray of cookies. "You promised you'd read me a story."

"I'm sorry," she said, dashing at the tears that trickled down her cheeks. "I've got to go."

Not giving him a chance to protest, she grabbed her coat, shrugged it on, and headed out into the cold. She paused and turned. Waiting, maybe.

For a moment, Dave's gaze softened. She was so lovely, standing there, snow-flakes dusting her hair. Her eyelashes glistened with them. It was all he could do not to raise his hand and brush them away.

She spun around, the jerky motion nearly causing her to slip. She caught herself in time and hurried to her car.

He made a move to stop her, but then he realized he couldn't change anything.

A small force charged into him. Startled, he looked down to find Justin pounding on him.

"You made her go away!" Pint-size fists pummeled his legs.

Dave scooped his son up and held his flailing arms and legs still. He carried Justin to the sofa and tried to cuddle him but was met with a solid wall of resistance.

"You ruined everything." A tear spilled over onto Justin's cheek. Pain stretched across his face, and Dave felt his insides twist. "You made her mad at us. Real mad."

"She's not mad at you," Dave said, picking his way carefully. *Just me*, he told himself. "She's still your friend. She'll always be your friend." With those words, he realized he'd spoken only the truth. No matter how angry she was with him, Katie would never turn her back on Justin.

"You made her cry."

The wobble became a full-blown sob. Dave started to draw his son into his arms, but Justin jerked away.

Finally, he succeeded in pulling Justin to him. The small shoulders beneath Dave's hands shook as sobs overtook Justin. Hurting because his son was hurting, Dave could only hold him and wait for the storm to pass. And pray that someday Justin would forgive him.

Justin poked at Dave's chest with an accusing finger, the gesture reminding him of Katie doing the same thing only minutes ago. "You don't know anything. You don't know anything at all. You made Mom go away and now you made Mith McGuire go away too." With that, he fled to his room.

Stunned by the accusation, Dave stopped in his tracks. Justin had barely been two when Marie left. How much did he remember? Obviously enough to make Dave the villain of the piece.

Slowly, he followed, only to be confronted by a closed door. From the hallway, he could hear the muffled sobs.

His heart ached for Justin. He might as well admit it . . . it ached for himself as well. Hadn't he known getting involved with a woman would lead to this? Savagely, he wadded up the torn piece of wrapping paper.

He'd known the risks of letting Katie into their lives, and he'd gone ahead with it anyway. Now Justin was paying the price.

The next morning, Justin was careful to sidestep any mention of the night before. Dave tried to get him to open up, to talk about his feelings about Marie's desertion, and was painfully reminded of Katie's suggestion that he do that very thing. But Justin remained stubbornly silent on the subject. He also refused to talk about Katie.

For the first time Dave could remember, his son pulled away from him. He was alone in every sense.

Easing Katie from their lives was harder than he'd imagined. He knew what needed to be done. Doing it was another matter.

When he suggested they make their annual trip to see the Christmas lights in the city on Saturday, Justin immediately asked, "Can we invite Mith McGuire? Maybe she's not mad at us anymore."

It was the question he'd been trying to avoid. "I don't think so this time, pal. She's probably got other plans."

"Maybe we ought to wait."

Dave couldn't believe what he was hearing. Going to see the Christmas lights in the city had been all that Justin could talk about for weeks. "I thought you wanted . . ." His voice trailed off as he saw the stubborn set of Justin's mouth.

"Okay, we won't go Saturday."

"Can we go next week? Maybe then Mith McGuire can go too."

"I don't think we ought to be spending so much time with Miss McGuire."

"But why?"

Why? The eternal question of children. He'd made it a practice to try to answer all of Justin's questions honestly and openly. When Marie had left, Dave had told Justin that his mommy had to go away. When the inevitable question came of when she would come back, Dave said she wouldn't be coming back. Not ever.

When Justin needed to have his tonsils out and asked if it would hurt, Dave had explained that it would hurt a little bit and he'd have to go to the hospital. He'd never shrunk from the truth, because lies hurt even more.

But now he was avoiding the truth. The stakes were higher now. He'd known going in that a relationship with Katie would probably end in pain, and he'd gone ahead with it. Now Justin was paying the price for his father's selfishness.

"Hasn't it always been just you and me for the last four years?" Dave asked, the touch of desperation in his voice sending off a warning bell. He recognized it from the first few months after Marie's desertion. "Haven't we had fun by ourselves?"

"Yeah, but . . ."

"But what?"

"I like Mith McGuire. She's pretty. And she smells good. And . . ." His lower lip poked out.

"And what?"

"Nothing."

"We can't plan our whole lives around Miss McGuire," Dave said at last.

"Why?"

"Because she might not always be here."

"Why?"

"Because she had a life away from here, one she may go back to."

"But she likes it here. She said so."

"Sure she does. That doesn't mean she'll stay here forever."

"If you ask her to, she will."

A child's faith was a humbling thing. There were some things, though, that even a father who loved his son as much as he did couldn't change.

"It's not that simple," Dave said.

"Wh—"

He held up a hand, cutting off the question. He didn't know if he could handle one more *why*.

But Justin wouldn't be stopped for long. "Why don't you want Mith McGuire to stay?"

"It's not up to me." Dave heard the edge of impatience cutting through his voice. He took a deep breath and tried to understand how things must appear to a child. The world was confusing enough for children without the adults in their lives playing games.

"You don't like her," Justin accused. "You said you did, but you don't."

He liked her all right, Dave thought. Liked her too much for his own peace of mind.

He made sure they kept busy over the next few days. A sleigh ride downtown, a trip to the roller-skating rink, a Saturday matinee of the newest holiday movie — they did them all. Justin went along with every suggestion, growing increasingly withdrawn with each activity. He tried. Dave would give him that. His son tried, but his heart wasn't in it.

Dave had a pretty good idea where his heart was. The same place as his.

With Katie.

Justin rubbed at his eyes with the heel of his hand. He didn't like crying. Tyler said crying was for babies. But sometimes, like now, he couldn't help it.

His dad had wrecked everything. Unless something happened real soon, Justin wouldn't be getting Miss McGuire for his mom. Not for Christmas or for any other time.

He knew he couldn't depend on Santa Claus to do all the work. Dad always said that if you wanted something, you had to work at it. The more you wanted it, the harder the work.

Justin didn't mind hard work. Especially if it meant getting Miss McGuire for a mom.

Chapter Eight

Monday morning, Katie put the finishing touches on the gingerbread house that the class had spent the last three weeks making. The children were as excited over it as they had been about the Christmas program.

Panting a little from an energetic game of kick-ball during recess, she hurried to her classroom. The whispering she heard from the hall halted abruptly as she walked inside.

The gingerbread house lay in pieces, the candy trim crushed into multicolored slivers. She turned to the class. A glance from her quelled the snickers and giggles that had started up again. "Who did this?"

A small raised hand caught her attention.

"Justin?"

He stood. "I'm sorry, Mith McGuire." He sounded sincerely repentant, but she couldn't ignore this.

"I'm going to have to call your father."

"Are you gonna ask him to come here?"

Her gaze went from the crumbled remains of the gingerbread house to Justin.

Her heart twisted at the pain she saw in his eyes. The idea of seeing Dave again wasn't helping matters either. "I have to."

The last thing she wanted was to cause more problems between father and son, but Dave had the right to know what had happened. Whatever existed between Dave and herself, they had an obligation to find out what was troubling Justin.

"Tomorrow?"

"If he can make it."

She looked forward to the meeting and dreaded it in equal parts.

A note requesting a meeting to discuss Justin's latest misbehavior was the last thing Dave expected — or needed — after an already dismal day. He'd thought that whatever had been bothering his son had disappeared. Now he knew he'd only been kidding himself.

"I'm meeting with Katie — Miss McGuire — after school today," Dave told Justin the next morning.

"Really?"

Dave frowned at the eager note in his son's voice. "The three of us are going to talk about what we can do to help you."

"Oh."

Something in Justin's expression

snagged Dave's attention. Why was Justin so eager for him to meet with Katie? Pieces started fitting together. "All these things . . . you did them on purpose, didn't you?"

Justin nodded.

"Why, Justin? Why?"

"I want Mith McGuire to be my mom."

Not sure he'd heard correctly, Dave took his time in framing the next question. "You wanted Katie to be your mother?"

"I asked for her."

"You asked for her?"

"I asked for Mith McGuire for my mom."

Though he'd entertained such ideas himself, Dave hadn't realized his son shared the same ones. "Have you told Katie — Miss McGuire — that?"

"No. It wasn't time."

"Wasn't time?" He was in over his head, Dave realized. Way over.

"Christmas is still a week away," Justin said with the patience of explaining something simple to someone feebleminded. "Santa Claus was going to bring Mith McGuire to us."

"Bring her to us?" He was trying, Dave told himself. He really was. His befuddled brain couldn't make sense of the words.

"Santa Claus was going to make her my mom."

"Oh." The pieces were starting to fit. Justin's insistence that his Christmas present was already taken care of. His reluctance to tell Dave what he wanted. "*That's* what you asked Santa Claus for."

"Yeah." Justin's lip wobbled. "But now he can't. 'Cause she hates us."

"The rabbits and breaking the gingerbread house — all that was to get me and Miss McGuire together?" He spoke slowly, trying to understand.

"Yeah. Mith McGuire is the mom I asked for," Justin said as his tears dissolved into hiccups. "She has happy eyes and a pretty smile. Like the angel on the top of the tree."

"You can't ask for a mom for Christmas," Dave said gently. "You know that."

"No I don't. I want a mom." The tears were gone, but temper remained. The small chin jutted out defiantly.

"Remember last year when we said that Santa Claus can't bring you everything you ask for?" Dave asked.

"Yeah." The word was grudgingly given.

"Well, a mom is one of those things Santa can't bring."

"Why not?"

Dave knew a wild desire to laugh. All that worry over Justin's adjustment, and all his son had wanted was to get Dave and Katie together.

It was so simple. Why hadn't he seen it before? And why hadn't he understood how deep Justin's desire for a mother ran? It seemed there was a lot he didn't know.

Like how to let go of the past and let himself love again.

He pulled himself from his thoughts when Justin said, "I thought if you saw her, you'd like her and want to marry her. She's pretty and smart and likes kids.

"I want a mother," he concluded. "Just like the other kids have."

Dave felt a sigh shudder from him. He'd done everything he could to take Marie's place, but obviously it wasn't enough. As hard as he'd tried, he couldn't make up to his son for the loss of a mother.

He gathered Justin close and kissed him. "I wish you could have told me."

"I wanted to, but I didn't know how."

That afternoon, Dave explained things to Katie.

"That's why he did all those things?" she asked. "Cutting the doll's hair, putting the rabbits together, destroying the ginger-bread house?"

"I'm afraid so."

"I see." The expression in her eyes was

so wistful that he had to fight the impulse to take her in his arms. Holding her even for a moment wouldn't solve anything and would very likely complicate an already impossible situation.

"I don't think there'll be any more problems," he said, needing to fill the stretch of silence.

"No. I don't suppose there will."

"Katie . . . if things were different . . ."

The steady gaze she leveled at him shamed him out of what he'd been about to say. Things didn't have to be different. *He* did.

Katie managed to hold back the tears until she made it home. There, she let them have their way, but they brought no relief. Neither did the darkness as she slid into bed three hours early. She closed her eyes, willing sleep to come and heal the lonely places in her heart.

Sleep couldn't do the impossible, though, and she pressed the heels of her hands to her eyes as the wretched tears started up again.

The past had a lot to answer for, she reflected. It kept Dave from recognizing love. It kept her from giving the love she so desperately wanted to give. It kept Justin from knowing a mother's love.

She and Dave had something special between them. If only he'd given them a
chance . . . if only he believed in them as
much as he clung to his fear.

"What's wrong between you and Katie?"
Dave's mother asked without preliminaries
when he picked up Justin the following
evening.

"Good to see you too, Mom." While
standing on the welcome mat, he stomped
the snow from his shoes.

"Justin says you made her cry." She
huffed a bit even as she offered him a mug
of hot chocolate.

"She's moving back to Chicago."

"You sure about that?"

"As sure as I need to be."

"What does that mean?"

"It means I can't let Justin be hurt. Not
again." He cradled the mug between his
palms, letting it warm them as he waited
for her next volley.

Never shy to speak her mind, she let him
have it. "Who're you trying to protect?
Justin or yourself?"

He reminded himself that his mother
was looking out for him just as he did for
Justin. "You don't know what it was like
when Marie left." He stopped. Of course

she remembered. His parents had always been there for him, were still there for him. Still, he felt compelled to defend himself. "He cried for her for weeks, asking when Mommy was coming back. I won't put him through that again."

Her voice gentled as she laid a hand on his arm. "Katie's not Marie."

He remembered Katie saying the same thing.

"She loves Justin." Her lips lifted in a smile. "She even loves you, though I can't think why."

"How do you know?"

She gave an exasperated sigh. "You've only got to look in her eyes to see what's in her heart."

She was right. Katie's eyes could no more lie than her lips.

"Why don't you tell her you love her and ask her to stay?"

He'd asked himself the same question and hadn't liked the answer he'd come up with. He was afraid.

"If you let her go, you're a bigger fool than when you let that woman get her hands on you."

Dave had no trouble in sorting out his mother's mixed pronouns. He'd been thinking much the same thing himself. He hadn't any right to ask her to stay, especially after the way he'd lit into her. He hadn't any rights concerning her at all, he thought with disgust. He'd made sure of that with his stupid edict against involvement.

"Well, what're you going to do about it?"

Absorbed in a mesh of thoughts, he looked up blankly. "What?"

"Katie. What're you going to do to get her back?"

He didn't have an answer to that. "I don't know," he said honestly.

"Tell her you acted like a jerk and beg her to forgive you. Then ask her to marry you."

The voice came from the sofa where his father had been lying, a newspaper tented over his face. "That's what I did with your mother when she refused to marry me," he said from beneath the paper.

Dave turned to his mother. "You refused to marry Dad?"

"You bet I did."

"Why?"

"He'd stomped off in a jealous fit when he saw me talking with another boy. Said I was flirting with him." She snorted. "As if I didn't have the right to talk with anyone I pleased."

Dave smothered a grin and waited

164

for her to continue.

"The next night he had the nerve to show up and ask me to marry him. I told him he was a bigger fool than my mother had always called him if he thought I'd marry a man who didn't know the difference between talking and flirting."

His father pushed himself up to a sitting position. "She gave me a tongue-lashing like you wouldn't believe." He winked at Dave. "Gets it from her mother."

Another snort, louder this time.

"So what happened?"

His mother took up the story again. "I sent him packing and told him not to come back until he could act like a gentleman."

"What'd you do, Dad?"

"I showed up the next night with a dozen roses, a two-pound box of candy, and a diamond ring. I had to get down on my knees and beg her to forgive me. While I was down there, I asked her again to marry me."

A smile of reminiscence brushed his mother's lips. "This time I said yes."

"After she kept me on my knees for a good long time," his father added.

"How come you never told me all this before?"

"Didn't think you'd be interested," his father said in his practical way. "Now you are, so we told you. Women like to hear the pretty words that men have such a heck of a hard time saying." He eyed his wife fondly. "It's worth it, though. Pretty soon, you find you even like hearing them yourself."

Still reeling from his parents' revelations, Dave wasn't prepared for Justin's stand-offish attitude when he wandered into the room. An attempt to hug his son met with resistance, Justin's small body going rigid in his arms.

"He wants Katie," his mother mouthed to Dave over Justin's head.

I know, his eyes telegraphed back.

Once home, Dave tried talking to his son, asking him about school, what he wanted for dinner, anything to get a response.

Justin's barely mumbled replies made it clear he wanted nothing to do with his father. After making a cursory attempt at eating the meat loaf Dave had thrown together, Justin asked to be excused.

Dave looked with distaste at his own barely touched meal. Weariness was catching up with him. Too much worry, too many sleepless hours, were taking their toll. He forced himself to take a bite and then another, not feeling hungry but knowing he needed the food. By keeping his mind carefully blank, he managed to finish most of the meal.

He thought of all the chores that needed his attention. The laundry needed doing, the kitchen floor hadn't been mopped in weeks, and old newspapers littered the living room floor. Right now, he couldn't even bring himself to clear the table.

Instead, he shrugged on a coat and wandered outside. The swirling snow had stopped, blanketing the ground with a layer of white. The night, as black as his mood, was clear. He pretended to study the stars, but their brightness mocked him. He shifted his gaze to the muted colors of Christmas tree lights shining from a picture window in the neighbors' house.

Katie would like the ever-shifting patterns the dancing lights cast on the fresh snow. Funny how many things reminded him of her. Icy pricks stung his face, the wind cut through his flannel shirt, and all he could do was think about her.

He headed back inside, determined to make his peace with Justin. A knock at the bedroom door yielded an unwilling, "Come in."

Dave pushed open the door and saw his son bent over his desk, his small body covering whatever he was working on.

"What're you doing?"

"Making a Christmas present," came the muffled reply.

"Yeah? Who for?"

Justin mumbled something that sounded like "none of your business."

"Is it a secret?"

"Yeah."

Dave felt a tingle of pleasure. Obviously, his son was making him a present. Maybe things between them weren't as bad as he'd feared.

"Guess you can't tell me what it is, then?"

"No."

The flat, uncompromising answer had Dave frowning and questioning his first guess that the present was for him. "Is it for someone special?"

"Yes." The reluctance was back. "Mith McGuire."

The breath knocked from him, Dave wondered why he was surprised. In Justin's eyes, Katie was the heroine of the piece; he was the villain. He tried to put aside his hurt feelings and concentrated on why he was there.

"I thought maybe you and I might grab a hamburger and then catch a movie," he said, ignoring Justin's eight-o'clock bedtime.

"No, thanks."

"Maybe some other time."

"Maybe."

Dave backed out of the room, hurting more than he thought possible. It wasn't that Justin was making Katie a Christmas present. He'd expected that. It was the secretiveness, as though his son couldn't trust him with the knowledge. It was the fact that the gap between them was growing bigger with each day.

Why didn't he admit the truth? Justin wasn't getting over Katie any more than he was, and it didn't appear that things were going to change anytime soon.

His mother was right. He was a fool.

Justin chewed on his lip as he thought about what his grandma had said to his dad tonight. Grown-ups acted dopey sometimes, he decided. Why couldn't his dad see that he and Miss McGuire belonged together? Then the three of them could be a family.

It was up to him to do something about it. Justin didn't doubt he could fix whatever was wrong. Hadn't his dad always told him that he could do anything if he set his mind to it? There was nothing that Justin wanted more than for Miss McGuire to be his mom.

Now all he had to do was figure out how to make them see that they needed each other. And that he needed both of them.

After cleaning her already clean apartment, Katie puttered about, watering plants that didn't need watering, plumping pillows that didn't need plumping. The shrill of the phone startled her from the empty tasks.

"Miss McGuire," a vaguely familiar voice said on the phone. "This is Sally Chase — Justin's grandmother."

"Of course, Mrs. Chase. How are you?"

"I'm not calling about me," the older woman said bluntly. "It's about Justin."

"Is something wrong with him?"

"Yes."

Katie's heart skipped a beat. "An accident? Where is he? I'll be there — "

"He's fine." A tiny pause. "Physically."

"I don't understand."

"Can we meet somewhere?"

"Well, you see, things are sort of . . . unsettled . . . between your son and me."

"My son's a twit," Mrs. Chase said.

A strangled laugh escaped before Katie could prevent it. Hearing Dave's mother call him a twit was the last thing she expected.

"It's important, or I wouldn't ask," the

older woman said, her voice gently insisting.

"Well . . ."

"For Justin," she added persuasively.

"All right. Do you want to come here?"

"That would probably be best."

Fifteen minutes later, Sally Chase arrived, a surprisingly young-looking woman with frankly gray hair and a comfortably plump figure. In her running shoes and cherry-red jogging suit, she looked like anything but a typical grandmother.

After introductions were exchanged, Katie waited for Sally to start.

The older woman took a moment to study her. "You're even prettier than Dave said."

"He said I was pretty?"

"No. He said you were beautiful."

The secondhand compliment flustered Katie. "Dave said that?"

"And a lot more." With that, Sally smiled. "As you might have guessed, Dave's not given to pretty words. But he feels things deeply." Her smile disappeared. "Maybe too deeply.

"After Marie left, Dave had to become both mother and father to Justin. He stopped everything but going to work and being with Justin."

"Mrs. Chase," Katie began. Because her voice came out sounding like the squeak of a rusted hinge, she paused and cleared her throat. "Mrs. Chase — "

"Sally."

Katie acknowledged the correction with a smile. "Sally, I know what you're trying to say, but — "

"Justin loves you."

"I love him too."

"What about Dave?"

"With all due respect, ma'am, I don't think that's any of your business."

Instead of being offended, Sally appeared pleased. "You love him. Good."

"I don't think you understand — "

"I understand. You're in love with my son. And he loves you."

"He does?"

"Of course he does. Why do you think he's behaving like such a fool?"

The question left her nonplussed. Sally Chase didn't pull her punches, Katie thought.

"He's so tied up in knots that he can't think straight. He's got you confused with Marie."

"I'm not Marie." Katie flushed as she realized she'd all but shouted the words.

"I know that. And deep down so does Dave. But he's terrified of letting himself love again."

"Where does that leave me?"

"That depends on you. Where do you want to be?"

In Dave's arms. With Justin tucked next to her side. The image was so vivid, so real, that Katie had to shake her head to dispel it. The way things stood now, there'd be no happily-ever-after for the three of them. Not together, at any rate.

"I appreciate what you're trying to do, Sally . . ."

"But it doesn't change anything."

"No. It doesn't." She'd told Dave how she felt. The next step had to be up to him.

Sally patted her shoulder. "When you're as old as I am, you get to where you don't care about pride."

"It's not a question of pride."

"Isn't it?" Gently Sally patted her arm before letting herself out.

Chapter Nine

Methodically, Katie graded papers, making comments and corrections while the children completed their seat work. When she discovered she'd marked the same paper twice, she decided she'd better take a break. Grading over thirty papers was enough to turn anyone's brain to mush.

Honesty forced her to admit the real cause of her inability to concentrate.

It wasn't the papers.

It was Dave.

She knew that he'd been hurt. Well, who hadn't? What right did that give him to accuse her of playing with his feelings? She'd never hurt him. Or Justin. Dave had to know that.

Underneath the anger was pain. She'd thought they shared something special. Whatever was between them, though, wasn't strong enough to stand up to some test Dave had imposed upon her. She only wished she knew what the test was. Maybe then she could pass it.

She knew Justin was confused. No more confused than she was, though. They both loved his father, yet Dave was determined to push her away.

"Miss McGuire, how come you don't smile like you used to?"

Emilie's question had Katie looking up. She made a conscious effort to curve her lips upward and prayed it would pass for a real smile. A look at Emilie's face told her she hadn't succeeded.

"I've had a lot of things on my mind," she said, knowing how lame the excuse sounded.

"Are you getting tired of waiting for Santa to come? My mom says she can't wait for Christmas to be over."

This time Katie's smile was genuine. With six children to care for, Emilie's mother was probably feeling overwhelmed by all the holiday preparations.

"Your mother works very hard," she said gently.

Emilie nodded. "I know." She gave Katie a curious look. "Will you be happy again when you get those things off your mind?"

Katie thought about it. "I hope so." She made a promise to herself that she wouldn't let her gloomy mood affect how she treated the children. They deserved her best.

The last day of school before the holidays was a flurry of excited whispers and last-minute touches to the children's presents for their parents.

When it was time for recess, Katie slumped down at her desk, glad to let the teacher's aide take over. Her throat felt raw whenever she swallowed, and she'd blown her nose so much that she could pass for Rudolph.

"Mith McGuire?"

She looked up to find Justin waiting for her attention.

"Are you still mad at Dad and me?" His small voice sliced through the misery that had settled over her like a gray cloud.

"I'm not mad at you," she said, feeling her heart break a little more. She flashed him a grin, but it felt stiff upon her lips. "See? I'm smiling."

Rather than being teased from his somber mood, Justin continued to fix her with an unblinking stare. "That's not a real smile."

The reproach in his voice wiped the fabricated smile from her lips. "You're right. It's not."

"Then why'd you do it?"

Good question. She picked her way carefully through the minefield of a six-year-old's reasoning. "Sometimes grown-ups do things they really don't feel like doing."

"Why?"

Another good one. "Because we're not very smart."

"Oh. Here. I made this for you." He placed an obviously child-wrapped gift in her hands.

Her hands trembling, she opened it and had to work hard to keep the tears back. Most of the children had brought her gifts — homemade treats, hankies, stationery. Justin's was a lopsided clay heart with his initials scratched into it.

"Thank you," she said when she'd conquered the lump in her throat.

"Do you really like it?"

"I love it," she said solemnly. "I love you." She hadn't meant to say that. Justin was confused enough about their relationship without her adding to it.

Still, she couldn't regret saying what was in her heart. Just because Dave couldn't accept her love didn't mean his son suffered from the same malady.

"What about Dad?"

"Your dad's a very special man." She fought back the tears that threatened whenever she thought about Dave. "What happened between him and me doesn't change how I feel about you." She gave him a hug. "Now it's time you get back to work."

He returned the hug. "Okay."

She managed to make it through the rest of the day with a fair semblance of her usual smile. When some of the kids stopped to wish her a Merry Christmas on their way out, she was hard-pressed to hold back the tears. Their sweet smiles put her own to shame.

She bit back a relieved sigh when the last of the children filed out. She'd miss them over the two-week vacation, but right now she needed solitude. The effort of keeping a smile in place had cost her.

Back in her apartment, she shed her holiday cheer as she peeled off her coat. With nobody to keep up the pretense for, she was able to sulk all she wanted.

The apartment with all its red and green decorations mocked her mood, and she scowled at the grinning Santa Claus who adorned her door. Two presents, the video game for Justin and sweater for Dave, nestled under the small tree that sat on an end table.

An invitation from an old college roommate to spend the holiday with her had Katie tempted. She could get away, put some distance between herself and Dave. There was nothing more lonely . . . or pitiful . . . than spending the holidays alone.

Before she could change her mind, she

called up her roommate and accepted the invitation. If her friend noticed Katie's lack of enthusiasm, she was too polite to mention it.

Katie tried to picture the holidays without Dave and Justin. The image refused to take shape. When she got back from the holidays, she'd put all this behind her and start again. She'd already turned down the offer to return to her old school in Chicago. Just because things hadn't worked out with Dave didn't mean she was going to give up the life she'd made for herself here in Canfield.

The townspeople were friendly, generous, and always ready to lend a helping hand. If their concern sometimes translated into prying, well, that was part of the charm of small-town living.

She loved the children in her class and liked being part of a school where everyone pulled together. There was no politicking as there'd been in the bigger, impersonal school she'd come from. No jockeying for plum assignments or backbiting in the teachers' lounge.

If only Dave . . .

She clamped down on that before she could complete the wish. Thoughts of Dave always seemed to be accompanied by treacherous tears that she couldn't control.

She missed him. She wasn't too proud to admit it. She missed both of them. And she missed Dave's slow smile, the one that took its time working its way up from his lips to his eyes. And Justin's gap-toothed grin that stretched over his face, sending the freckles across his nose dancing.

Smiles hadn't been part of her life lately. She'd found little to smile about. That was no excuse, of course. Smiles eased the little hurts of life, and she'd been stingy in giving hers away — one more thing she had to correct before the start of the new year.

Of course she'd never had to deal with a broken heart before. With Todd, her pride had taken longer to heal than her heart. She'd put the broken engagement out of her mind with embarrassing speed. She had a feeling it was going to take far longer to put Dave out of her mind. And even longer to put him out of her heart.

The following day, she finished a few chores around the apartment before taking off to visit her roommate. When her car refused to start, she'd called an auto service and learned she had a dead battery. The serviceman jump-started her car and then presented her with a hefty bill. She thought that had been the end to her troubles.

She'd been wrong.

After doing a bit of last-minute shopping, she discovered she'd run out of checks and had to leave the things she'd selected at the store. She'd returned with her checkbook and paid for the purchases.

Sulking wasn't her style. Right now, though, she felt she was entitled to a major sulk. A case of the sniffles that had been brewing for the last few days had blossomed into a full-blown cold, not helping matters any.

Maybe a nap would restore her energy, if not improve her mood. The bed beckoned invitingly, and she slumped onto it without even removing her clothes. Two hours later, she awoke groggy and fuzzy-mouthed. A glance in the mirror confirmed that she looked nearly as bad as she felt, with a nose red from blowing it and sleep-matted hair.

A glance outside confirmed that it was too late to start the trip. With little regret, she called her friend and begged off.

Rummaging through her refrigerator, she came up with a half gallon of peanut-brickle ice cream. The cool treat soothed her sore throat, and she worked her way through half the carton of ice cream before her stomach protested at the overload of sugar.

She shed her clothes and pulled on an old terry robe that should've been relegated to the rag bag years ago. It hugged her like an old friend, and she snuggled deeper into its comforting warmth.

The phone was blessedly silent. Friends had given up asking her to their holiday parties. She made up so many excuses that she'd tangled herself up in them, unwilling to face the prying eyes and whispered comments that were sure to accompany her presence at the parties.

The advantage and the curse of small-town living were one and the same: everyone knew everyone else's business. That the new elementary teacher and the town's most eligible bachelor had broken up was bound to be top news.

Justin glanced at his grandpa, who was snoring loudly, his head propped against the armrest of the sofa. The controls to the Nintendo game they'd been playing dangled from his hand.

Gently, Justin shook him. "Grandpa, wake up. We're not done yet." He leaned closer. Wow, his grandpa had really gross nose hairs. They stuck out a long way, practically a whole foot. A thunderous snore caused Justin to jump back.

He wandered over to the window and peered outside. He was bored. Grandma had gone to the store, so he couldn't ask her to play with him.

If Miss McGuire were here, she'd think up something fun to do. She had the best ideas of anyone he knew. He was going to miss her during the next two weeks of Christmas vacation.

His dad said Miss McGuire wouldn't be coming around any more and they just had to get used to it. Justin didn't *want* to get used to it. He wanted her to be his mom. He'd been real good the last three months in an effort to earn this one wish from Santa Claus. But then his dad had gone and wrecked everything.

Maybe if he told her that his dad wasn't really mean, she'd come see them again. Justin knew she loved him. She'd told him so just yesterday.

He knew she loved his dad too. And his dad loved her. He'd seen the way the two of them looked at each other when they thought no one else was watching — all funny and goony-eyed, like the pictures on the covers of the books his grandma liked to read.

If she loved his dad and he loved her and Justin loved both of them, he didn't see why they couldn't be a family. Grown-ups made things hard when they didn't have to be. Like now.

He figured all he had to do was get Miss McGuire and his dad talking. He'd heard his grandma say that they belonged together, that they were just too blind to see it. Justin wasn't sure what the last part meant, but he understood about his dad and his teacher belonging together. Grandma thought so too. She was old, so she knew what she was talking about.

That was it. He'd go see his teacher and tell her. His grandma had shown him how to buy a bus ticket. All he had to do was know where he was going.

He had to find out where Miss McGuire lived. His dad had taught him how to look up addresses in the phone book. Carefully, his finger following the lines in the Mc section, he found his teacher's name. Tearing the page from the book, he wadded it up in his pocket. He ran into his room and dumped the contents of his piggy bank on the bed. He stuffed the money into his jeans pocket.

Standing on a chair, he grabbed his coat and mittens from the closet. He was ready.

When the phone rang, Dave was

tempted to ignore it. He had specs to go over for a new product design. The last thing he needed was another interruption after a day full of them.

Reluctantly, he picked it up, propping the receiver between his shoulder and his ear while he scanned the report from product development.

"Dave, is Justin there?"

It was his mother's voice, rather than her words, that snagged his attention. "He's not with you?"

"No." The word snapped with impatience. And something more. Fear. It crackled over the line even as it crawled along his nerve endings. "If he were, I wouldn't be calling you."

"Take it easy, Mom. Tell me what happened."

"I had to run to the store. I left your dad and Justin playing Nintendo. When I got back, your dad was asleep on the couch and Justin was nowhere to be found."

Don't panic, Dave ordered himself. He wouldn't help anyone by going off half-cocked.

"Have you checked outside?" he asked, his voice carefully controlled. "In the basement? The garage?"

"We've looked everywhere. I put off

calling you, thinking he'd show up. But he hasn't."

"Okay. Let's take it slow." He had her repeat exactly what happened, absorbing the details and trying to keep the fear from his voice. "Why don't you and Dad alert the neighbors, ask them if they've seen anything."

"Dave, I'm so sorry." Tears made his mother's voice thick. "If I'd thought . . ."

"I know, Mom. It's not your fault." He swallowed past the lump of terror in his own voice. "I'll head home and see if he's there."

They both knew Justin wouldn't go home by himself. Ever since Marie had left him by himself, he'd been terrified at the idea of being alone in the house. Even though he'd been little more than a baby at the time, he still remembered.

Where else would he go? The question throbbed inside Dave's head as he broke every speed limit on his way home.

The house was empty, as he'd known it would be.

Fear knotted in the pit of his stomach and coated the inside of his mouth with a coppery taste. He shook it off; he couldn't afford the deadly paralysis that too frequently accompanied panic. He needed all his energy focused on finding Justin. Nothing mattered, nothing would ever matter again, as long as his son was all right.

"Please," he prayed. "Please let him be all right." His words, torn from his heart, startled him into action.

A call to his parents confirmed that Justin hadn't returned. He scrambled through a drawer looking for the school directory. He started with Tyler, calling each of Justin's friends until he'd worked his way down the list. Each call met with the same answer. No, they hadn't seen Justin. Yes, they'd call if he showed up.

Only one place remained. The fear was now a living thing, licking at his senses until he was all but paralyzed. Katie lived on the other side of town. If Justin had tried to get to her, he'd have to cross any number of major streets.

Dave pushed aside the images his mind conjured up all too easily, each picture more horrible than the last. Even a small town wasn't immune to the evils of the modern world.

The prayers tumbled out, one upon another. In the end, there was only one. *Let Justin be all right.*

When the doorbell rang, Katie muttered

something about people who didn't know it was too late to come calling. Tightening the belt of the robe around her waist, she headed to the door, barely missing the two small bags she'd packed for her trip.

A momentary pang gripped her as she remembered Dave's warning about opening the door before she knew who it was. Seemed like just about everything reminded her of Dave these days. Pushing thoughts of him from her mind, she swung the door open to see an unfamiliar woman holding Justin by the hand.

"He says he needs to see his teacher," the woman said. "Are you the one?"

Katie managed to nod while stooping to pull Justin into her arms. "Thank you. Thank you so much."

"I'm glad to help." After a gentle admonishment to Justin not to go off by himself again, the woman waved good-bye.

Lips blue with cold, he shivered visibly even as his lips spread in a wide smile.

"Come on." Katie scooped him up into her arms. "What're you doing here?" she asked as she tucked him under an afghan on her sofa.

"I'm visiting you," he said proudly between the chattering of his teeth. "I came on the bus."

"How'd you know where I live?"

"I looked it up." He reached in his pocket to pull out a much-folded page from the phone book. Her name and address were underlined. "I asked the bus driver which bus to take and he told me. He dropped me off, but then I got lost and I asked the lady how to get here."

She caught his hands in hers and held them. "It's all right now," she murmured, holding him close. "Why did you have to see me tonight?"

"I want you and my dad to stop being mad at each other."

"We're not mad — "

"You are too. Dad said you didn't want to see him anymore. I heard him tell Grandma that you might be moving back to Chicago."

"I'm not going anywhere."

"You're not?"

"Uh-uh. I'm staying right here." Justin needed her. And whether Dave knew it or not, he needed her too. If he was too hard-headed to see what was staring him in the face, then she'd have to make him see it. She'd never been a quitter and she didn't intend to start now.

But first she had to tell him Justin was here. A gasp caught in her throat as she realized how panicked he must be. She started for the phone, only to have her steps halted by the doorbell. Sharp jabs betrayed impatience, and she picked up her pace, already knowing who was there.

"Justin's gone." Dave, his face harsh in the hall light, panted out the words. "I thought he might have — "

"He's here," she said gently.

The tears in his eyes had her blinking back ones of her own. Whatever the differences between them, they shared a love for the little boy who was even now throwing himself into Dave's arms.

Dave ran his hands over his son, as if to reassure himself that Justin was indeed all right.

"Dad, are you real mad?"

"No, pal." Hands trembling, Dave hugged Justin to him, holding him as if he'd never let him go.

Feeling out of place, Katie started to back out of the room when Dave caught her wrist. "Stay. Please."

She looked uncertainly from him to Justin. The little boy let go of his father to slip his hand in hers. "Don't go, Mith McGuire."

As usual, the sound of her name in his lisping voice melted her heart. He tugged at her hand, pulling her down on the sofa beside him. She had pictured the three of them like this — arms around one another, a family bound together by love if not by blood.

"Why did you run away?" Dave asked when long moments had passed.

Justin looked surprised. "I didn't run away. I had to see Mith McGuire. So I took the bus to see her. Like Grandma showed me."

"Grandma showed you how to get to Katie's house?"

"No. But she took me to the doughnut shop one time and I saw how she gave the driver money. So I told the bus driver where I wanted to go. He helped me find the right bus."

His child's faith in the goodness of others shamed all the horrific pictures her mind had immediately called up upon learning he'd taken a bus clear across town. A look at Dave confirmed he'd shared the same fears.

"Why did you have to see Katie . . . Miss McGuire?" he asked.

"To ask her not to be mad at us anymore."

The simple answer had Katie and Dave looking at each other and then quickly looking away.

Justin yanked at her hand. "I'm hungry."

"How does soup sound?"

"Chicken noodle?"

"I think I can manage that." She turned to Dave. "How 'bout you?"

"Maybe a little later. I need to make some calls, let everyone know he's all right."

"Phone's on the table." She gestured to a large steamer trunk that served as an end table.

He called his parents first and then asked his mother to let the others know Justin was safe, all the while aware of Katie and his son in the kitchen. He heard Justin's high-pitched giggles and Katie's soft answering chuckle.

It was so simple, he wondered why he hadn't seen it before. The two people who meant the most to him loved him. For reasons that no longer made sense, he'd tried to deny Katie's feelings and selfishly keep his son all to himself.

He was a thickheaded jerk who'd allowed himself to be a prisoner to the past for long enough. If she'd still have him, he intended to ask her to marry him.

Then he saw them. Two suitcases stacked neatly by the bedroom door. By the looks of them, packed and ready to go. Had he waited too long?

With a glance at Justin, who was busy slurping down his second bowl of soup, Dave motioned for Katie to follow him. In the cramped pantry off the kitchen, he pulled her to him. And held her there.

He didn't say anything, unsure of the words to keep her there. He could beg her not to go, but was that fair to her if she'd made up her mind to return to Chicago?

He pulled the towel from her hair and ran his fingers through damp curls the color of dark gold. He felt as though he'd waited forever. For her. This moment. This rightness.

It hadn't been merely weeks since he'd last seen her, held her in his arms. Misery wasn't measured in days or weeks. It was counted in the hours, the minutes, that they'd been apart.

To heck with being fair. He needed her. Here. With him and Justin.

He'd known from the start, an inevitability even as he'd fought against it, a half-formed wish that had only taken one look at her to fall into place. His hands slipped to her arms, urging her closer.

"I love you, Katie."

The words she'd longed to hear failed to fill the cracks in her heart. She tried to pull away only to find her arms held fast.

"Don't," she begged. "Don't say it if you're not sure. I don't think I could handle it if you sent me away again."

"Do you think I could?" He cupped her shoulders, his hold possessive yet infinitely gentle. "You and Justin and I . . . we belong together. I think I've always known. I was just too much of a coward to admit it."

She waited. She wouldn't make it easy for him. The words had to come freely, without pressure on her part, if they were to mean anything.

A sigh rippled from him. "I wish I could wrap it up in a pretty package. The fact is, I'm a selfish jerk. It's been just Justin and I for so long, I didn't want to let anyone else in."

"You're right. That is selfish. And stupid."

"Yeah. Otherwise I'd have known you would never hurt us."

His hands were in her hair, on her face, holding her close enough that she could feel the uneven thump of his heart, hear the quickening of his breath, smell the male scent that was uniquely his.

When she stepped back to study his face, she saw the need that she knew was reflected in her own eyes. "You were trying to protect your son."

The temptation was great to take the easy out she'd given him. No, he wouldn't lie to her. Not any longer. His fear had been for himself. Justin had a child's faith in the goodness of people. He'd seen what Dave had refused to: that Katie had an abundance of love to give. She gave it unstintingly, with no thought to the cost to herself. She gave it because that was the way she was.

For almost four years, he had let the past control him. It had nearly cost him a second chance at love. He couldn't afford to let it cost him Katie.

"I was protecting myself. I thought you'd go away, that you'd leave us alone, like . . ."

"Marie?"

"Yeah. I knew you were nothing like her, but I wouldn't let myself believe it. I wouldn't let myself believe you cared enough to stay."

"You were an idiot."

He nodded ruefully. "I kept hiding from what I felt, afraid if I admitted I cared, I'd be vulnerable again, The night of the Christmas program, I realized I loved you. I was going to tell you and then I saw the letter." Guilt colored his voice, but he kept his gaze level with hers.

"You read my mail?"

"I didn't mean to. I saw something about you returning to Chicago. Before I knew what I was doing, I . . ." He shrugged. "It was the perfect excuse to push you away. I told myself it was for Justin.

"I couldn't control what I felt for you. I promised myself I'd never feel that way again. When I realized I did, I was scared."

"Why didn't you ask me?"

"I didn't *want* to know the truth. If you were leaving, it meant I'd been right all along. If you weren't, I was left trying to figure out what I felt for you."

"Now's no different than then," she felt bound to point out.

"I'm different. It took Justin to teach me that love's worth taking a chance on." He captured her hands in his. "Don't leave me, Katie. Don't leave us. We need you."

"Both of you?"

"Both of us. Marry me, Katie. Be my wife and Justin's mom."

Wife and mom. Such simple words.

Gently, she pushed him away, framing his face with her palms, needing to see if he truly meant what he said. She searched his eyes and found only honesty. And such love that it took her breath away.

"Come home with us," he said. "We'll call

my parents and tell them the good news."

She thought of her red nose and tangled hair. "Only a man would suggest I go out when I look like this."

"You're beautiful. You always look beautiful to me."

How could she refuse a man who claimed she looked beautiful when she was wearing her rattiest robe and fighting off the effects of a cold?

The answer was simple: she couldn't.

"I've loved you forever. I just didn't know it. Can you forgive me for being a fool?"

Her kiss was answer enough as she threw herself into his arms and found his lips with her own. "Don't ever let me go," she whispered.

"As if I could."

Two days later over Christmas dinner, Dave watched as Katie helped Justin serve pumpkin pie and ice cream to his grandparents. A warmth settled over him as the image imprinted itself in his heart.

As if sensing his gaze on her, she turned and looked at him. He crossed the room to join his son and the woman he hoped to make his wife. When her hand slipped inside his, he knew he'd come home.

Epilogue

Red and green lights twinkled along the entrance to the hospital, reflecting off the snow that blanketed the ground. Dave carried a huge white bear and an even larger bouquet of red roses.

"Hurry up, Dad," Justin called impatiently, tugging at his father's hand. "I want to see Noelle and Katie."

Dave pretended to pant as he stepped inside. "Give your old man a moment to catch his breath."

"You're not old," Justin declared loyally. "Not real old. Grandma says you're still in your prime, even if you do have two kids."

Dave chuckled. In his prime. Maybe his mother was right. He had a beautiful wife, a wonderful son, and a brand-new daughter.

Inside the hospital room, he bent to kiss Katie's cheek. "How're my two best girls?"

"Hungry." She gestured to their daughter, who suckled noisily.

Dave caught his breath at the picture they made as light haloed their heads. He bent over to kiss Katie and then stroked

Noelle's velvety cheek with the pad of his thumb.

"Here," he said, handing a grease-stained sack to Katie. "Your favorite." He lowered his voice. "Don't tell the nurse I sneaked it in."

She pulled out a double cheeseburger and extra-large sack of fries. "Thanks. You saved my life. If I had to look at one more bowl of lime Jell-O . . ." She shuddered.

Justin eyed his baby sister with something akin to awe.

"How'd your program go?" Katie asked, using her free arm to hug him.

"Great. I was Rudolph. I brought my nose to show you." He thrust a circle of red construction paper in her face.

She chuckled. "I bet you were the best Rudolph in the second grade. Next year Noelle and I'll be there to see you."

"I brought you a present." He held out a sack.

She looked inside and found gumdrops. "Thank you. Just what I wanted."

"This is the best Christmas ever," Justin said.

"You said that last year," Dave reminded him.

"Last year we got Katie in the family. This year we got Katie *and* Noelle."

★ ★ ★

Dear Santa,

Katie and Dad say I have to rite thank u notes for my presents. Thank u for the computer you bringed us. It's neat. And thank u for Noelle. She spit on me but I still like her.

Love,
Justin

PS Next year could you bring me a brother?